Mitzvah

CLAW & WARDER

Episode 3

Erik Henry Vick

RATATOSKR PUBLISHING

NEW YORK

RATATOSKR PUBLISHING
2080 NINE MILE POINT ROAD, UNIT 106
PENFIELD, NY 14526

MITZVAH/ ERIK HENRY VICK. -- 1ST ED.
ISBN 978-1-951509-06-4

TABLE OF

CONTENTS

Chapter 1 1
Chapter 2 29
Chapter 3 233
Chapter 4 259
Chapter 5 269
AUTHOR'S NOTE 277
ABOUT THE AUTHOR 281

For Jennifer DuBrava Hinton, my nemesis.

I hope you enjoy *Mitzvah*. If so, please consider joining my Readers Group—details can be found at the end of the last chapter.

CHAPTER I

THE BODY

In the magical justice system, magically based offenses are considered bad form.

In the Locus of New York, the dedicated teams of supernatural detectives who investigate these breaches of Canon and Covenants are members of an elite squad known as the Supernatural Inquisitors Squad.

These are their stories.

I

Sarah Jane cursed under her breath. She cursed the scarf that refused to stay tucked in; she cursed the wind that tugged at the scarf and splattered her face with fat, wet snowflakes. Sarah cursed the three brown paper bags she had to schlep back from the bodega three blocks away—all because the governor had banned the use of plastic bags. Plastic bags *and* their convenient handles. Her mood had grown as foul as the weather and grew darker with each step, as did the sky. The fact that the bodega had been out of toilet paper and Kleenex—the two items that had gotten her out in the oncoming storm to begin with—had made her feel ready to commit murder.

Her scarf slid from around her neck and danced away into the gloaming. "Bastard wind!" Sarah yelled.

The wind howled in reply.

Sarah ducked her chin into the collar of her coat and kept on, her face pointed at the sidewalk to keep the wind-borne ice from gouging her cheeks and eyes. *At least I'll have a nice dinner and a hot toddy*, she told herself.

Something pelted into her from the alley as she crossed in front of it. Something dark and big. As she fell toward the ice-choked gutter, the thing that had sent her flying snarled but kept right on trucking. She hit the street with an explosion of air from her lungs and the cacophony of her groceries thumping and rattling onto the macadam.

She pushed herself up onto her elbow. "*You fucking bastard!*" she shouted.

At the end of the block, the dark figure stuttered a step and straightened as it slid to a halt. It turned toward her, greenish-gold eyes gleaming in the low light. The dark figure's mouth dropped open, and it emitted the most horrible noise she'd ever heard—a noise that froze her mid-movement and seemed even to stop her heart. It was akin to a dog snarling at someone it hated, only ten times worse.

Sarah scrambled out of the gutter, scrabbling against the cold pavement with her gloved hands and the heels of her winter boots, backing madly away from the thing in the intersection. She clambered backward until she slammed into the unforgiving stone wall of the building behind her. The monster in the street hunched its shoulders and took a single step toward her, and Sarah screamed, throwing her hands up to cover her eyes.

When she worked up the courage to splay her fingers and peek through them, the beast was gone. Breathing a sigh of relief, Sarah covered her mouth with a gloved hand and shuddered for a moment. She climbed to her feet, still watching the intersection like a cat watching a dog, and then bent to retrieve her purchases.

She re-bagged what had survived the fall, kicking the broken or destroyed items into the gutter. *At least I only have two bags to carry now.*

Sarah gathered her packages in her arms and stepped back onto the sidewalk. As she did so, she glanced into the alley from which her antagonist had bolted. The evening grew darker with each breath, but not so dark she couldn't see the mess near the dumpster.

She took a single step into the mouth of the muck-strewn alley, then dropped her groceries for the second time, turned and bolted for her apartment, screaming like a tea kettle at full boil.

She no longer noticed the cold wind.

2

Leery Oriscoe held his cup of coffee carefully as he idled the unmarked car forward until it tapped the bumper of the Prius at the end of the block. He gunned the accelerator and pushed the little car forward with a shriek of protesting tires. He didn't stop until the Prius sat in the intersection, and then he put the Crown Vic in reverse and backed into the recently vacated last spot.

Dru shook her head. "Just going to leave that poor car out there in the street?"

"Poor car? That's a *Prius*, Nogan." He sipped his coffee and popped his door open. "Come on. The scene's right down the block."

Shaking her head at the small car standing alone in the intersection like a forlorn lover on a train station platform, she got out and belted her coat around her middle. "One day, Oriscoe, you're going to catch hell for something like this."

"Yeah? That's okay. I know someone related to one of the Four Queens of Hell. I'm sure she can help me out."

"What makes you think I'd speak to my mother on your behalf?"

"Oh, you thought I meant you?" Leery flashed her a saucy smile, then turned and walked down the sidewalk. "Come on, Princess," he called over his shoulder.

Muttering curses to hide her grin, Dru followed him.

Ahead, Leery ducked under the yellow crime scene tape, then stopped for a big swig of coffee. As she crossed under the tape herself, Dru wrinkled her nose. "What's that smell?"

"Hear that, Sergeant Briggs? That is an example of the keen senses you have to cultivate to make it into SIS."

The officer keeping the log looked at him and arched her eyebrow. "Aren't you dead yet, Oriscoe? You've got to be, what, ninety?"

"Oh, Patricia, that stings!" Leery downed the rest of the coffee and held the empty cup out to her. "Here, I wouldn't want to dirty up the scene."

Patricia Briggs tilted her head to the side and glared at him for a moment, then turned to Dru. "Can't you house-break him?"

Dru scoffed and shrugged. "Can't teach an old dog new tricks."

"Ouch! Two age jokes in such proximity! A guy could get a complex." Leery stood there staring at Briggs, holding out his empty cup until the officer shook her head and took it. He grinned at her. "I'll take another, thanks. As big as you can get around here."

"I'm the officer of the log, Oriscoe. I can't just—"

"No, I drink it black, but thanks anyway," he said, talking over her. "Hey, I really appreciate you running down to that bodega in this weather. That's really going the extra mile." He turned away from her, ignoring her outraged expression, and stepped to the mouth of the alley. "Over here, Nogan. Come see what your nose already found."

"You can shoot him if you like," said Dru.

"I would, but I don't want the paperwork. You want a cup?"

"You don't have to do—"

"Yeah, but I'm already going for your flea-bitten partner."

Dru shrugged. "Yes, please. A small, with seven sugars."

Sergeant Briggs arched an eyebrow at her, then shook her head, mumbling something about diabetes. Then she turned and walked over to a patrolman and sent him for the coffees, adding a cup for herself.

Dru turned and followed Leery into the alley, trying not to breathe through her nose. The alley smelled like a slaughterhouse—the unmistakable coppery odor of blood, the scent of a ruptured bowel, the reek of raw meat. "What do we have, Oriscoe?"

"Oh, not much for a Thursday night." He turned back to her and stepped closer. "Looks like something went a little nuts on this poor woman."

Dru pulled out her flashlight and painted the scene with blue-white light. Something had shredded the poor woman's abdomen and chest and ripped out her throat, festooning the bricks with her blood. "Hellfire," Dru muttered.

Leery grimaced. "You can say that again."

"Any ideas what did this?" she whispered.

Oriscoe grunted and darted a glance over his shoulder at the mouth of the alley. "Yeah, unfortunately. These wounds...the throat, they spell one thing to this old wolf."

Dru glanced at him.

"Yeah," he said in a tone she could only just hear. "One of my kind."

3

They climbed the stairs to the third floor in silence, wet snow becoming wet slush as the ambient heat of the building did its work. Leery heaved a sigh. "Why can't people live in buildings with elevators? What's the apartment, again?"

"Briggs said 4F."

"Four Feh!" He flashed a sardonic grin her way.

Dru took a dainty sip from her small cup of coffee and pretended not to notice the grin.

"You going to drink that, Nogan, or just wet your lips?"

"If you hadn't dashed yours down in one gulp, you'd have some left, too."

"Hey, it was a tiny cup."

"It was twenty ounces, Oriscoe."

"Yeah. Like I said, tiny."

Dru treated him to a lopsided smile. "Want some of mine?"

"What, ruined with seven sugars? No thanks." Leery heaved another sigh as they rounded the mid-story landing. "Ten more steps, Nogan. Just ten more."

"Think you can make it?"

"Carry me?"

Rolling her eyes, Dru pushed past him and climbed to the top of the stairs. She looked right, then swung around and pointed to the left. "4F."

"Right, right." Leery plodded up the steps and followed her down the hall. "Ms. Jane?" he called as he knocked on the door to 4F. The deadbolt clanked, and the door opened to the extent of the chain. "It's Detectives Nogan and Oriscoe."

"I already told everything to that sergeant," said Sarah Jane.

"She takes lousy notes," said Leery. "Chicken-scratch."

"It would help if we could hear the story firsthand," said Dru.

"Well..." The door closed, then reopened without the chain. "I guess you'd better come in."

"We appreciate it." They followed her inside the tiny apartment and stood on the linoleum floor in the entryway. "We understand you've had quite an evening already."

"Hey, you wouldn't have any coffee brewing, would you?"

Dru chucked her elbow into his ribs. "Can you tell us what you saw earlier this evening?"

Sarah blanched and raised a slow hand to cover her mouth. "It was...*horrible*. That woman..." She shuddered.

"Yes, it was a terrible thing," said Dru. She stepped toward Sarah, but the other woman took a step back.

"Briggs told us you saw something running out of the alley?"

Sarah turned her wide-eyed gaze on Leery, then shook her head. "Not then. I was walking back from the grocery up the street, and as I came next to the...the alley, somebody knocked me down."

"Somebody?"

Blood filled Sarah's cheeks, and she dropped her gaze. "Uh, yes. He knocked me asprawl and—"

"Asprawl?" echoed Leery.

"I'm a reader...I like to read. I picked it up from a book."

"It's fine," said Dru and glared at her partner.

"When I... When I got up, he was already to the intersection. He... He made a noise... I was... I was scared, and I averted my gaze."

"Think you can describe him?"

"No!" She jerked her head left and right. "I mean, I didn't get a good look." She dropped her gaze.

Leery and Dru exchanged a glance.

"Listen, Sarah," said Leery. "We investigate strange things all the time."

Dru nodded.

"Stuff you wouldn't believe. We know there are weird things in this city. Scary things."

Without raising her head, Sarah peeked at them. "Really?"

"Sure. All the time. So, if you saw something that, well, you might be embarrassed to tell us about..."

She swallowed hard. "I'm not sure *what* I saw. It's more what I heard."

"What you heard?"

"Yes. It—*he*... He gruh-growled at me, I think. It made my blood run cold."

"Why did you pick that word? Growled?" asked Dru.

Sarah lifted one shoulder slowly. "Because that's what it sounded like. Like one of those devil-dogs from the horror shows. You know, the black and brown ones?"

"Sure," said Leery.

"And his eyes..."

"Glowed in the dark? Like in a photograph?"

"Yes. Green. No, gold. They glowed gold." She locked her gaze on Leery's face. "What was it?"

"Oh, no doubt about it." Leery trotted out the smile he had used when he'd told his daughters there were no monsters under the bed. "Some sicko out to terrify you so you couldn't remember his face."

"Well, it worked."

"I'd like to have one of our artists come by in a bit and work through a sketch with you."

Sarah shook her head. "I really didn't see him."

"Sure, I know," said Leery. "But these sketch artists are really good at jogging memories. Teasing out little details you probably don't realize you know."

Again, Sarah lifted her shoulder.

"It would really help," said Dru. "We could stay if you want."

"No, I know you need to be out there looking for him." Sarah sighed and settled onto the couch. "Send your artist. I'll try my best."

"Terrific," said Leery. "It will be a huge help."

4

Back on the sidewalk outside Sarah Jane's building, Leery hunched his shoulders against the wind and blowing snow. "You make the call. Have them send Johnny. He's always good with the girls."

"Sure thing." Dru fished her phone out of her pocket and stepped back into the foyer of the building.

Leery continued down the sidewalk, squinting against the blowing snow and frigid temperatures. If it hadn't been so windy, there might have been a scent trail to follow, but as things stood, they needed a break.

As he neared the alley, Jenn Hinton came stomping out of it, her bag of tricks slung over her shoulder, her scarf wrapped around the lower part of her face. "Hey, that's a great look for you, Hinton."

"Oh, hello there, Scooby. I wondered when you'd show up."

"Are you done playing with your little candles and drawing with sidewalk chalk?"

Hinton rolled her eyes. "Why, did you want to color, too?"

"I'm glad they sent you, Hinton. At least I can share this wonderful weather."

"Aw, with friends like you, a girl could wish for death."

"A girl? Maybe. An old demon like you? No way."

"Now you've gone and hurt my feelings, Checkers."

Leery grinned, and Jenn smiled back. "What did you find back there?" He hooked his thumb at the alley's mouth.

"Looks like someone's dinner," said Hinton with a shrug. "Her spirit's too far gone to get anything out of her. Too much trauma."

"Isn't there some kind of treatment for Ghost Traumatic Stress?"

"Very punny, Ambrosius. But to answer your question, no. If we're lucky, she'll settle down in a decade or two. If we're not"—Jenn glanced over Leery's shoulder at the shadowy alley and shrugged—"well, let's just say that alley might be a phantastic place."

"Boo," said Leery with a frown.

Jenn shrugged. "Everyone's a critic. Say... Where's your coffee?"

"Yeah, I know. The world is a cruel place." Leery glanced down the street as Dru stepped out of Sarah's building. "We're going to have

Johnny Smith do his little parlor trick with the wit."

"The echoes in the alley are pretty intense. I'll tell him to be careful."

"Wouldn't the echoes be from the victim?"

Jenn put her hand on her hip. "You'd think so, but in this case, the victim was already out of her head. Your witness took a big fright, and the living leave stronger psychic impressions than the dead." She turned to her CSI van and slid the side door open. "As fun as it is to stand around in this wind with you, Leery, I'm going home."

"Braggart."

"See you tomorrow." She grinned at him as she climbed inside the van.

"Not if I see you coming, nemesis."

5

L eery hung his coat on the rack, whistling the theme from Scooby-Doo. When he turned around, Van Helsing hovered behind him.

"I don't have any Scooby Snacks," she said with a trace of a smile.

"Good thing. They're gross. Not like coffee."

Dru puffed out her cheeks and hung up her own coat. "Hinton called him Scooby. He's been singing the damn song ever since."

"Yeah, it's a catchy tune."

"Hell has no tortures to match it," said Dru.

"You would know," said Leery with a smile.

"Cute," said Van Helsing and rolled her eyes. "What do you have?"

"Female. Mundane," said Leery.

"Butchered. Eaten," said Dru. "The wounds look like a wolf made them."

Epatha shot a glance at Leery.

"Hey, don't look at me. My wolf has me keeping kosher."

"Hinton?"

Leery shook his head. "The victim was too traumatized."

"Imagine that." Van Helsing crossed her insubstantial arms. "And I hear there was a witness?" She glanced at Dru.

"Yeah. She's who we needed Johnny's services with. He should be here soon," said Leery.

"He's already back."

Dru shot a glare at Leery. "I *told* you."

"I was cold. Coffee warms me up."

"He's in my office," said Van Helsing with a crooked grin. "They invented this neat thing back when I was young, Leery. It's called a vacuum flask. It keeps things hot."

"They call them Thermoses, now, Lieu. And I really have to call bullshit. You were never young."

"Shut up, Oriscoe," she said. "Let's go see what Johnny has for us." She turned and floated toward her office.

"Be right there, Lieu."

"I already have a cup for you in my office, Leery."

"It's nice to be loved," he said, falling into step with Dru as they followed Van Helsing across the squad room.

As they entered the room, Johnny Smith stood up and grinned at Leery. "Hey, you old dog."

"Hey, yourself, Johnny. Get anything from Sarah Jane?" He shuffled past Johnny and picked up a giant mug of coffee from the desk and slurped some down.

"Yeah. She saw a werewolf, alright. A big one, too."

Leery grimaced but said nothing.

"Did you pull any details from her memory?"

Johnny dropped his gaze and sat down. "Yes. And it doesn't make sense. It *can't* make sense."

"What doesn't make sense, Johnny?" asked Van Helsing.

"Well, a couple of things, but the biggest thing is that I..." He tossed a quick glance at Leery, then cut his eyes away.

"Spit it out, Johnny," said Leery. "We're all friends here."

"The werewolf was waiting for her."

"For the victim?"

Johnny shook his head. "For Sarah Jane."

"What?" asked Dru.

Smith nodded. "That's right. He stood just inside the alley's mouth. He watched her struggle up the street. He waited until she was in front of him, then charged right into her. He *meant* to knock her down."

"How do you know that?" Dru glanced at Leery and cocked her eyebrow at him.

"We all see far more than we pay attention to. Right now, even though you're not looking at me, you see every move I make. Every expression. But you ignore all the extraneous information in favor of what you are focused on. It was the same thing with Sarah this evening. When I viewed her memories, however, *I* paid attention to all those things."

"*That's* the big thing that doesn't make sense?" asked Leery with a grin.

"No. Uh, that is... Uh." Johnny gave in to a spate of nervous laughter. "It's... It can't be right. She misremembered, or the visit to her apartment muddled her impressions or something."

"Spit it out, Smith," said Van Helsing.

He glanced at her, then cast sheepish eyes at Leery. "She saw enough of the werewolf for me to see clearly. The wolf wore a black wool hat." He cleared his throat and looked at his feet. "It was Oriscoe."

"Well, now I've heard everything. Did Hinton put you up to this, Johnny?"

Johnny raised his face, gaze locked steadily on Leery. "No one put me up to anything, Leery." His voice was quiet but firm.

"But that's crazy," said Leery.

"There was a time, Leery," said Van Helsing.

"Not for years, and never like this," snapped Leery. "I always had my ticket."

Epatha nodded and held up a placating hand. "And in any case, you were working when this happened."

Leery grimaced and looked down at his shoes. "I need an alibi, now, Lieu?" His voice was quiet but bristled with fury.

Van Helsing arched a single ghostly eyebrow at Dru.

"He went for coffee. Came back with one, too."

"Right, and I was gone, what, five minutes?"

"Ten, maybe," said Dru.

"So, I ran a hundred and seventeen blocks, committed a murder, staged a close call with a witness, then ran back in ten minutes? Come on, Lieu."

"No one's saying that, Leery, but this begs an explanation. The wounds, they weren't faked, were they?"

Leery grimaced. "No, those cuts looked real enough."

"And you would know," said Epatha. "So, we have an unlicensed, unsanctioned werewolf killing"—she held up her index finger and began ticking off her points, one by one—"a witness that undoubtedly saw the doer, a poor woman who happened to be in the wrong place at the wrong time—"

"We don't know that, Lieu," said Dru.

"Right, but we *will* find it out," said Van Helsing. "And she remembers a werewolf that

Johnny recognized as you. What about the victim? Who was she?"

Dru flipped open her pad and read from it. "Preliminary identification is one Kay Soper, of Alphabet City. We got that from a discarded purse near where the body was dumped." She raised her gaze to Leery. "No idea if that's who she really is. The IDs can be faked as we all know, but the ME is running the aura trace against her records. She said she'd have results by tomorrow morning."

"Kay Soper? Are you sure about that, Nogan?" asked Leery.

"Yes."

Leery shook his head and grumbled something no one could hear.

"What is it, Oriscoe?"

"I knew Kay Soper. We grew up in the same neighborhood. She and Dee Terry were pals all through school." The room settled into an uncomfortable silence for a moment. "I know how that looks, but I haven't seen Soper since high school."

"Fine. For now, see if Kay Soper and your witness knew each other, Dru."

"And what about me?" asked Leery in a querulous tone. "I haven't seen Kay Soper since the eleventh grade, and Dee's disappeared into witness protection."

Van Helsing rotated her entire body to face him. "You know what I have to do, Leery," she said in a low voice. "Don't make it ugly."

"Ugly? Why would I make it ugly?" A rictus settled on his face. "I'm not riding a desk."

"Don't be that way, Leery," said Van Helsing. "I can't keep you on the street. You know the regs as much as I do."

"Yeah, I just thought you knew me as well as I know you." Leery pulled the leather case that held his badge from his pocket and dropped it on the floor. "There. Now, I guess I can go home."

"I'll keep it until you want to take it back, Leery."

"Right."

"And I'll make sure this is paid and won't go in your file. You've got vacation time."

"Thanks for that, at least." He turned and walked to the door. "And thanks for the coffee, Lieu. See you later, kid."

"I'll clear you, Leery. I promise," said Dru, putting her hand on his arm.

"If you want my opinion, I'd start with Rose Marie Van Dee."

Dru watched Leery breeze out of the squad room as if it meant nothing, but the tense lines of his shoulders and neck told a different story. She turned back to the lieutenant and opened her mouth to speak, but Van Helsing cut her off.

"No, don't even start," the lieu said. She turned her gaze on Johnny Smith. "Write up your report, please. For now, leave out the part about recognizing the wolf."

"But—"

"Do as I bid you, if you please."

Johnny shrugged and stood. "You'll have both versions of the report by tomorrow morning. What you do with them is up to you." He turned and brushed by Dru. "For what it's worth," he said without turning, "I don't think Oriscoe did it."

"Nor I," said Van Helsing. "But the forms must be followed." After Johnny left, she turned her attention on Dru. "Now, bricky miss, we'll see if you've learned anything from old Leery."

Dru lifted a hand helplessly. "Where do I start?"

"See if the victim and the witness are connected.

"Will Leery be all right?"

"Damfino," said Van Helsing. She turned as if she could follow Leery's progress out on the street. "He's poked up, and I've never seen him this angry."

6

Leery stopped by the motor pool and got his hat and the now-bent *menorah* from the trunk of their squad car. He kept his face under rigid control, but inside, he seethed with fury, and as was always the case when rage colored everything he saw, his wolf was very close. He had to bite down on the instinct to swipe with his claws, to snap his jaws and sink his fangs into any irritating soft flesh that got in his way.

He stormed out onto the sidewalk and then stopped. He closed his eyes for a moment and let the cold air and wet snow revive him and cool his temper. He needed his mind clear; he needed to think.

No way in Hell I'm staying out of this. I haven't worked this hard, sacrificed this much to the job to let someone set me up. He heaved a sigh. *Besides, what else have I got to do?*

Leery clamped his hand on top of his hat and turned into the wind. Then, he walked to the corner and hailed a cab.

CHAPTER 2

THE

INVESTIGATION

I

Dru Nogan closed her burning eyes. She only intended to rest them in a long blink but found it difficult to force them open. She hadn't slept—not so much as a cat-nap—and had spent the long hours of the night staring at her laptop screen and performing one database search after another. She knew she should have taken the opportunity to rest, to catch a little shut-eye in the precinct's room set aside for that purpose. Still, she was a night owl by nature, if not by upbringing. The truth of it was she didn't need to sleep, but she had grown accustomed to it—out of boredom more than anything else—and her body seemed intent on keeping up the habit.

She had been unable to find *any* link between Dee Terry and Kay Soper, and from what Leery had said, there should be school records, at least. She'd checked Leery and Dee and found records for the pair at Theodore Roosevelt High School, but for Kay Soper, nothing. Nor could she find property records for the Soper family anywhere in the Bronx.

Strange, she thought with a wry twist to her lips. *Here's a woman someone doesn't want to exist. But why? And who? And if they didn't want us to know who she was, why leave the damn purse with her ID in it?*

Dru forced her eyes open and peered at the clock in her laptop's status bar. The ME had promised to verify the identity of the remains first thing this morning, and Dru intended to witness the aura trace in person at 7:30. If she hurried, she could dip by a Skirt Club party for a light snack and still be at the ME's on time. The parties ran until sun-up, and she could sit in a dark corner and just drink in the lust.

She closed her laptop and went to get her coat. She felt a vague sense of guilt about taking the time to eat, but she had to maintain her energy, or she might lose control. At least this way, she wouldn't have to rely on hot blood.

2

As the sun peeked above Long Island and shimmered across Long Island Sound, Leery stood amidst a thicket of trees in Mamaroneck, staring at Rose Marie Van Dee's McMansion. For the house of someone serving four consecutive lifetimes in the dungeon beneath Sing Sing, the place sure was busy.

He'd stood in the same place for most of the night, and his feet had begun to ache and cramp three hours before. But he wasn't going to move. Not an inch.

Vehicles had gone in and out of the estate throughout the night, and all of them had been driven by zombies. For a moment there, he had questioned whether Rose Marie Van Dee was really locked away or not.

The house had been lit up like Times Square all night, and no one had bothered to close the shades. Leery had watched and learned and taken mental notes. Rose Marie had boasted that she could run her occult cabal from inside the dungeon, and by all appearances, the Van

Dee Family wasn't so much as slowed down by the inconvenience.

But still, is it Rose Marie running things, or is there a new player? Inside the house, there was one zombie everyone seemed to defer to—the zombie that spent most of her time on one burner phone or another. It wasn't clear whether she was running things or relaying orders from someone else. *I need to hear those calls, but a trap and trace is out.*

At least a legal one.

Leery didn't recognize the woman on the phone, but he hadn't worked the OC squad for years. Even so, he had friends in the bureau who could help—*if* they were willing to help a pariah, and *if* he could snap a picture of her without blowing the surveillance.

3

Liz Hendrix arched an eyebrow at Dru as she pushed through the swinging doors that connected the autopsy room and the public area outside. She stood by a stainless-steel table on which the mutilated remains of the woman found in the alley the night before rested. "Where's your dog?"

Dru grimaced. "He's taking some time off."

"What? Leery? No way." She glanced down at the body, her eyes tracking from the wounds in the woman's throat to the torn and lacerated muscles of her abdomen. "Don't tell me someone thinks Oriscoe did this."

"Why would you think that? Leery's just taking some vacation time."

"Riiiight," said Liz. "Well, it's stupid, and you can tell your ghost boss I said so. Leery's been clean a long time, and he wouldn't jeopardize that for a pound of flesh." She glanced at Dru, and their gazes locked. "Besides, who will bring me coffee?"

"Can we just get on with it? The sooner I can figure this out, the sooner your pet wolf can bring you coffee."

Liz flashed an obviously fake smile. "Sorry. I didn't realize I was holding you up." She pointed at the lab counter running the width of the room. "Stand over there so you don't screw this up." She turned her back on Dru and pulled a surgical instrument tray closer. Reaching above her head, she adjusted the angle of the brilliant lights to focus on the woman's torso, then moved the microphone's boom arm closer.

With a glance to ensure Dru had followed her directions, she crossed to a cabinet behind her. Liz withdrew a table-mirror-sized chunk of quartz that had been cut and polished like a gem, encased with silver, and marked with spidery silver runes. She placed the crystal on the surgical tray and stepped behind it. "Don't move," Hendrix instructed. She opened a chart and lay it next to the looking glass. Hendrix raised her hands and began to chant.

The sound of chant, the spidery language Hendrix used, and perhaps even the source of her power, made Dru's skin crawl. She gritted her teeth, resisting the urge to turn away, fighting the urge to vomit. The air above the woman's torso began to shimmer and pulse like heat devils dancing in the Nevada sun. Hendrix's voice rose to a fever pitch, and beneath it, Dru thought she heard the ME's chant double, then treble, as if unseen witches added their voices to the incantation. The voices were sweet and pure, like the tones of glass bells stuck with soft mallets, and Dru's nausea grew. *Angels*, Dru thought with an inward sneer. About the time Dru believed she would have to run into the hall, a cornucopia of colors and dancing shapes erupted over the body. Blues danced with yellows, greens with reds, browns and oranges, black and white.

Hendrix leaned close to her crystal looking glass and peered into it, then glanced at the chart. With a nod, she drew the chant to a conclusion, and the angelic voices faded, then disappeared completely.

"You could have warned me," Dru snapped. "I didn't know you were one of *those*."

Liz flashed a crooked smile. "One of those? One of what?"

"A holy roller."

"My, but you live a sheltered life, Princess," said Liz with a shake of her head.

"Does *everyone* know?" Dru murmured.

"I use whatever spells are called for. Whatever *power* is willing to listen and help. You should try it. Expand your horizons. Oh, that's right..." She cocked her head to the side. "You can't, can you?"

Dru grinned and widened her eyes. "Perhaps you should be careful. One of those powers you mentioned might become...less interested in helping you."

"Your mother's not so petty."

"Isn't she?" Dru smiled sweetly. "I *am* her only daughter."

Hendrix paled a little as she stepped around to the head of the table once more, or maybe it was just the bright surgical light. "Yes, well... Maybe we got off on the wrong foot this morning."

"Perhaps so. Perhaps I should have brought coffee."

Liz glanced down at the remains on her table, and neither Dru nor she spoke for a moment. "I have good news, though. This woman is Kay Soper."

"Beyond any doubt?"

"Yes. Aura traces don't lie. They're better than DNA."

Dru nodded. "That's good and bad."

"Leery?"

"He knew someone named Kay Soper. Went to school with her in the Bronx about a thousand years ago."

"Eh, not quite that long ago." Liz frowned down at the corpse. "These wounds were made by a werewolf. There's no doubt of that, either." She stared at Dru, then stepped around to lean against the table, arms crossed under her breasts. "Tell me, Nogan. Maybe I can help."

Dru's lips twitched as she considered her response. "You know Johnny?"

"Johnny? Johnny Smith?"

"Yes."

Liz nodded.

"We sent him to talk to a witness under the guise of making a sketch. He sifted the woman's memories, and..." She frowned. "You may never read this part in an official report. Are you sure you want to know?"

Liz nodded. "For as much of a pain in the ass as he can be, Leery's...not as bad as being burned alive."

"Right. Johnny says he recognized the wolf in the witness' memory. He said it was Oriscoe's wolf."

Liz held up her hands as if to push someone away. "Not possible. Leery would—"

"I *know* that. But I have to *prove* it."

"Regs," Hendrix sneered.

"That's right."

"Epatha should know better!"

Dru cocked her head to the side and stared at the ME for a moment. "I think she does, but she's not one to bend the rules."

"Well, let's see what Soper can tell us. Maybe there is something you can use to exclude Leery."

"That's what I'm hoping," said Dru with a nod.

Liz turned back to the corpse and bent close to examine the bite marks around Kay Soper's neck. She muttered another spell, and power cracked in the air like a winter's worth of static electricity.

Dru grimaced and blinked away the tears brought on by the sudden stinging in her eyes.

"Look here, Nogan," said Liz, pointing at the bite marks. Rainbow colors danced in the wound like oil scumming the surface of clear water. "See this? This is the residue of black magic, but it's unlike anything I've seen before." She glanced at Dru. "Maybe it looks familiar to you?"

Dru shook her head. "I've never seen spell residue like this—or spell residue in general for that matter. But this feels... I'm not sure *feel* is the right word, but this feels familiar. Even so, I don't know this kind of magic."

"Must be something archaic. Something out of the mainstream."

"Something to do with the Pack?"

"No, nothing like what werewolves do, even when they are hybrid magic users. Their magic is more primal...more like the magic of native cultures."

"Nature-based?"

Liz nodded. "Not far distant from druidic spellcasting."

"I see. So, this isn't much help identifying the caster, but we could use it to nail him once we've found him."

"That's it in a nutshell."

"Perfect," murmured Dru. "Any idea what purpose the spell fulfilled?"

Liz cocked her head to the side and stared at the oily residue, pursing her lips. "It's hard to say. Let me do some research, maybe work this a bit more."

Dru nodded. "And Liz?"

"I know, I know. As soon as I can, Detective."

4

Stiff backed, thigh muscles shrieking in protest, Leery made his way out of the copse of trees in Mamaroneck, moving with a silent grace few could match, but paying for it. He'd stayed as long as he dared in the full light of morning. He could have let his wolf out and stayed longer—human senses couldn't touch him when he wanted to be a sneaky wolf—but he had the feeling he'd seen enough.

The image of the zombie in charge was burned into his memory. He couldn't learn anything else by watching her talk on the phone and shout orders at other rotting-flesh-sicles.

Back on Van Wagenen Avenue, Leery trudged up the shoulder to the shitbox car he'd rented on the cheap. Once there, he folded his large frame into the tiny vehicle, cursing car designers in general, and made his way back to more familiar territory.

He lived in a little apartment near Columbia. He wanted to change clothes, catch a quick shower, and make a few calls. He ignored the blinking light on the answering machine attached to his landline and plugged his cell phone in for a quick charge while he showered.

He stood in the hot stream of water for a long time, letting the heat work some of the kinks out of his stiff muscles. He always used a soap whose fragrance was supposed to wake a person up, and he inhaled the scent in large gusts as he lathered and washed.

Feeling somewhat better, he dressed for work. *Look the part,* he told himself as he tied one of his awful ties. He'd left his badge with Van Helsing, which, in hindsight, was stupid. Without it, he'd have to get creative.

If Van Helsing thought he was going to sit this out, to sit around watching stupid "reality" television while he was reality railroaded, she didn't know him as well as he'd thought. He froze in mid-knot, staring at himself in the mirror. *If you really believe Van Helsing expects you to hang out at home, you're nuts, Oriscoe. You know her better than that.*

The face in the mirror twisted with a crooked smile. He did know her better than that. And that was the reason she didn't ask for his badge and gun. She expected him to work the case—though her adherence to the regulations forbade her from saying so.

With a new spring in his step, he went back to the living room and hit the button on his answering machine.

Beeeep!

"Mr. Oriscoe? This is James down at the desk. A package was delivered for you by courier in the night. I'll have it for you at your convenience."

Beeeep!

"Leery, it's Dru. Listen, don't sweat this thing, okay? Liz found traces of a strange kind of magic in the wounds of the victim. I'm trying to trace it down, and we can use it to nail the bastard who did this. Okay? Call me."

Beeeep!

"Hey, wolfman, it's Deli. Where have you been? I need a good—"

Leery pressed the stop button, a small grin dancing around the corners of his mouth. He turned and went downstairs to the doorman's desk to get his package.

It was a padded manilla envelope with his address written in a scrawling Victorian-era script. His eyes crinkled with a suppressed smile as he tore it open. When he saw the black leather fold-over containing his shield inside, a wolfish grin blossomed on his face.

"Thanks, Jimmy!" he said as he stepped out past the doorman. He walked to the corner, where his rental car sat with two wheels up on the sidewalk in the crosswalk. He climbed inside and dialed Dru on his cellphone.

5

Leery parked down the block from the Starbucks and set off at a brisk pace for the place where he had agreed to meet Dru. A clunk and a scrape sounded from behind him, and he turned, then a wide grin spread across his face.

Dru had their Crown Vic bumper-to-bumper with his little rental coffin and was busily pushing it into the alley so she could steal his space. He stood there grinning until she looked his way, a smile twinkling in her eyes.

"About time you learned to park," he said.

She killed the ignition with the back half of the four-door Ford sticking out into the street and got out. "See that, Oriscoe? That's how a person should park in Manhattan. If you paid attention, you could learn a thing or two from me."

"Damn right, Nogan. Damn right." He waited until she joined him, then turned to walk to the coffee shop on the corner. "Although I'll never learn to like seven sugars."

"I can't ask for miracles."

"Well, I think *you* could, but that would take more than a miracle." He grinned at her as he held the door for her. "And maybe 'miracle' is the wrong word, eh? After you, Princess."

"Why, thank you."

Leery followed Dru inside, and they gave their orders to the barista: a tall coffee with seven sugars, and a *trenta*, black. They waited on their coffee, then found a matching set of wingback upholstered chairs near the windows. "Tell me what you've got."

"Like I said in my message, Liz found some strange spell residue."

"Yeah. We'll drop around later. I want to see it for myself."

"Sure. I also spent most of the night tracing Kay Soper's records—or *trying* to. She's a curious blank."

"I told you, Dru: we went to school together until the eleventh grade."

Dru nodded. "I found your records at Theodore Roosevelt High School, and records for Dee Terry, but nothing for Kay Soper. In fact, I can't find *any* records for Soper earlier than five years ago."

"No one can spring out of the womb as an adult. And I *know* Kay went to TRHS with Dee and me. She and Dee were pals."

"Right, and I believe you, Leery. But someone sterilized her records."

"That doesn't make sense. Why go to all that trouble to incriminate me, and then destroy the proof I knew her?"

Dru shook her head. "You got me there, Leery. Unless..." She sipped her coffee.

"Unless what, Nogan? Don't leave a guy hanging out in the wind."

"Unless it's not you that they want to break the link to."

"You mean Dee Terry? That link was broken by the Covenancy Marshalls."

"True, but maybe they had recent connections that someone doesn't want to come out in the open."

"You mean the zees."

Dru nodded. "Sure, I do. If Dee Terry was *Noster Est*, and if she and Soper maintained their relationship after Dee changed, then maybe Soper was affiliated."

Leery took a gulp of coffee and stared out into the gray morning sky. "Yeah. That gels." He returned his gaze to Dru's face. "I spent the night playing Peeping Tom over in Mamaroneck."

"Mamaroneck?"

"You bet. That's where Mama Rose Marie's house is."

Dru arced both eyebrows. "You peeped in the Van Dee family's windows?"

"All night. They're pretty busy for being completely gutted and boarded up. Cars and trucks and vans, in and out all night. And a nice dead girl on the phone until all hours, giving orders to the working stiffs."

"Who is she?"

"I have no idea, but I have a friend in OC who might help us with that."

Dru's face wrinkled. "The lieu shouldn't have taken your shield. You're far too valuable to waste like this."

Leery smiled and mimicked tipping his hat. "She didn't, remember? I'm the one who got all *verklempt* and stormed out. Besides, Lieu took care of me." He pulled out his badge and showed it to Dru. "Delivered by courier early this morning."

Dru smiled. "The old girl's not nearly the stiff-back I thought she was."

"She keeps up appearances, but she's got a deep rebellious streak."

"Practical, too."

"Tomato, tomahto."

"Is one thirty-two-ounce coffee enough, or do you need to get some to go?"

"And here I thought you were learning."

"Right, right. Go order. I'll run you by the ME's, then we can go to the OC bureau."

"Nah, let's hit them in reverse. We might have more information for Liz that way."

6

Leery pointed at a space about four feet wide between two small cars on Broadway. "Park here, Dru."

Shaking her head, Dru nosed the push-bars against the rear bumper of the little silver Yaris and pushed it forward. "Gonna get my ass in a sling," she muttered.

"Hey, let's leave personal lives out of this."

"Right," she said with a grin as she turned toward the window. "You *wish* I'd share those details with you."

"Uh," Leery said as he looked out his own window. "Evans said she'd meet us in the Starbucks on the corner."

"Yeah, that's why we drove all the way down here, Oriscoe." Dru twitched her lips to hide the grin that wanted to spread there as she backed away from the Yaris into the spot she'd made.

"Get your tires up on the curb so some asshole doesn't push you forward."

"Right," she said with a laugh and bumped the tires onto the concrete. "Come on."

They entered the shop, and Leery looked around for a moment before smiling and approaching a table. Yvonne Evans was a tall woman with strong features and somewhat wild hair that danced around her face like a drunken halo. She grinned up at Dru and held out her hand. "Call me Evie."

"I'm Dru."

"Is this old dog treating you right?"

Dru laughed and nodded. "Sure."

"You've got to keep him on a tight leash."

"Uh, I think I'll grab a coffee while you two get these jokes out of your systems."

"Oh, shut it and plant it, Oriscoe," said Evie with a wink toward Dru.

"Evie was my Warder when I was back in OC." Leery sank into one of the straight-backed cane chairs. "Did you bring the book?"

Evie rolled her eyes. "Give me strength. *Of course,* I brought them, Astro."

"I'm going to kill Hinton," Leery grumbled. "Is there anyone she hasn't infected with this?"

"Oh, be a good sport. You have to admit Jenn owes you after those posters you had made showing her wearing Mitzvah Tanks for shoes. I mean, the school buses were bad enough."

"I tried," said Leery with a smile. "And she did *walk right into those.*"

"Har-har. Ever think of a career in comedy?"

"Van Helsing already used that one. Tell Hinton she's got to *step up* her game."

"Oy. Quit while you're ahead, why don't you?" Evie reached into the black leather bag at her feet and withdrew a black binder. "Here, distract yourself with this."

"Right," said Leery. He flipped open the cover, found the tab labeled "Photos," and started leafing through the eight by ten images.

"Tell me, Dru. Is he still addicted to coffee?"

"I'm surprised he hasn't ordered a *trenta* yet, to be honest."

"Hey, a guy's got to have priorities." Leery turned a page. "Besides, I know those coffees on the table behind Evie are for me."

"Oh, poo." Evie turned and grabbed the tray from the table.

"You can't fool me, Evie. I'm a detective."

"Any luck with those pictures, *Detective*?" asked Dru with a smile.

"Nah. The zee's not in here. But I saw a lot of these street captains last night. They came in one after the other like there was some kind of interview process going on." He cocked his head to the side as if listening to a far-off siren. "Hey, you don't suppose Mama Rose Marie was telling the truth, do you?"

"About what?" asked Evie.

"Van Dee tried to make a deal with the Covenancy. She claimed she had set up a super-organization of families from different loci. Kind of a 'one ring to rule them all' thingy."

Evie raised her eyebrows. "And they didn't go for it?"

"Oh, they went for it," said Leery with a grin.

"I don't understand."

"McCoy," said Dru. "He kicked their asses in Covenancy court, and then Judge Gyuki blocked them from setting aside Mama Rose Marie's conviction in a Locus of New York court."

"But she also said she could run it from anywhere."

Dru nodded. "That's true, and we know she already corrupted one magister to play her games."

"That was the Angie Carmichael assassination attempt?" asked Evie.

"Bingo," said Leery.

"Come on, Oriscoe. That's too easy." Evie grinned and sang, "B-I-N-G-O, and Bingo was his name-o!"

"Oh, Evie," he said with hangdog expression. "That one really bites."

"Don't growl at me, Leery."

"You two quit barking at each other," said Dru.

Leery looked at her, straight-faced, and shook his head before hitting her with a wide grin. "That's the spirit. Just jump right in." He turned to Yvonne. "How do we find this woman, Evie?"

"Get a sketch together and send it to me. I'll circulate it as a possible captain in *Noster Est*. I can reach out to a friend in the Ceebies."

"Ew, the CBI... Look for it later today." Leery picked up the tray of coffees. "Thanks for the coffee, Evie. Great to see you again."

"Sure, help yourself, you selfish mutt," she said but smiled at the same time. "I poisoned one of them."

"Good thing I'm a werewolf, then." Leery turned and headed for the door.

"That man will never change," she said to Dru.

"Can't teach an old dog—"

"Nah. Don't waste it if he's not around to enjoy it."

7

They headed over to the ME's office, Leery still carrying the Starbucks tray of coffee. He caught Dru looking at it and held it out to her. "Want one?"

"Isn't that theft?"

"Nah. Evie will have paid for them."

"I mean the tray."

"Oh, this thing?" Leery glanced downward as if the tray's presence surprised him. "It's for customer convenience, right? I find it convenient to carry all these coffees. I only have two hands." He pushed through the double doors into the autopsy room. "Oh, Liz! I brought you coffee!" he called in a singsong voice.

"Hello, Oriscoe. What's shaking?"

"Dru tells me you have some magic goo you're having trouble identifying."

"That's true. It's a strange residue, to be sure. So far, I haven't come across anything quite like it. However, there are some similarities to the perversions of certain religious magics."

"Ah." Leery put the tray down on the stainless-steel counter lining the side of the room. "It's in the wounds?"

Liz nodded and picked up a tall cup of coffee. "Thanks for the Joe."

"Hey, anything for you, Hendrix."

Leery approached Kay Soper's remains, his nostrils flaring. "Strange..." He bent over the body and sniffed the wound at her neck. "Oh, there's something I haven't smelled in a long time."

"What is it?"

Leery straightened and turned his back on the corpse. "Smells like Kabbalah to me."

"What, Jewish mysticism?"

"It's more than that, Dru. You of all people should know that. After all, it was your mother who gave the secrets of magic to the sage, Amemar."

"Oh." Dru cut her gaze to the floor. "I don't know everything she's done."

"Of course, you don't," said Liz. "How could you? She's the Witch Queen and commands the Eighteen Legions."

Dru sniffed. "Yes."

"Then maybe she can help us trace this particular spell."

"I was hoping you wouldn't say that," murmured Dru. She raised her eyes and met Leery's gaze. "She won't come up. We'll have to take Soper's remains down."

"Oh! A field trip! How fun!"

"Can I tag along?" asked Liz. When Leery looked at her, she shrugged. "I've been intrigued by her story since I was a little girl. I'd love to meet her."

"Sure," said Dru. "Why not? She loves to meet her fans."

8

Dru opened the front door to her penthouse apartment and stepped inside. "Please come in," she said. She turned and dropped her keys, her badge, and her gun on the small table set near the door for such purposes and kicked off her low-heeled shoes.

Liz Hendrix gave Leery a glance and wagged her eyebrows, then stepped through the door. "Nice place," she said.

"Cripes, Nogan. How many people do you have living here?" Leery closed the door behind him with his free hand and stepped past Liz into the expansive granite-lined foyer. "I think this entryway is bigger than my apartment." Kay Soper's body-bagged remains were draped over his shoulder. It hadn't drawn *too* much notice in the lobby...

"Oh, it's just me," said Dru. "And I'm sure your apartment is much the same."

"On a cop's salary? Wouldn't that be nice."

Liz chucked her elbow into his ribs. "Will your mother meet us here?"

Dru shook her head. "No, we'll have to go to her. I've got a portal in one of the spare rooms."

Liz turned to Leery and mouthed, "She's got a *portal*."

"Hey, it beats the subway," Leery said. "Where does your mother call home these days?"

Dru turned back to him and quirked her eyebrows. "Where do you think?"

"You don't mean..."

"Come on, you two. Unless you need to use the restroom before we go? My mother has facilities, of course, but it's best you both stick close to me."

"I'm good," said Leery. "I've hardly had any coffee today at all."

He and Liz followed Dru across a gargantuan living room filled with modern electronics and comfortable furniture. They glimpsed the fancy gourmet kitchen as they passed it, and then walked down a long hall to the last door on the left, which Dru opened. Eldritch light danced on the walls from within, painting the hall with dancing ambers and reds as though reflected from open flame.

"Hey, listen, Dru. We're not going to...uh...meet anyone else, right?" asked Leery.

Dru shrugged. "Maybe Daddy will pop in."

"But, uh, no one higher up in the chain of command? Say a guy with hooves and a tail?"

"Uncle Luci?" She treated him to a coy smile. "No, when Mother needs him, she goes to him. It's only fitting."

"Yeah, uh... Yeah, I suppose so."

"You're not scared of my family, are you, Leery?"

"Well, no, of course not. I'm just... There are... I mean—"

Dru burst into bright laughter. "Relax, Wonderdog. Things don't always match the mythology around them. You can control your change, right? No full moon needed?"

"Well...sure."

"Uncle Luci's not the red-skinned, forked-tongue bugaboo from religious mythology. You'd like him. He's got that same smart-ass sense of humor."

"Oh."

"You'll understand better after you meet Mommy."

"Yes, I'm sure 'Mommy' will put my mind at ease."

"Come on, silly-bones." Dru turned and entered the room. "Oh, kick off your shoes, both of you. Mommy doesn't like them in the house."

"Uh, right," said Leery, setting Soper down and bending to pull off his glistening new Florsheim loafers. He stepped into the room, his gaze drawn to the large circle of dancing flames hovering inches off the carpet. "That seems like a fire hazard."

"It's *magic*, Oriscoe," said Liz. "It won't burn anything its owner doesn't want it to."

"Hopefully, that extends to werewolf partners." He squatted and cradled Kay Soper in his arms.

Dru dimpled. "You'll have to try it and see." She turned and stepped through the portal.

"Sometimes I don't know when she's kidding," murmured Leery.

"It amazes me the human race didn't die out long ago," said Liz. "Then again, I guess there were women around to make sure there were babies."

"What are you saying, Hendrix?" asked Leery, but it was already too late—she'd leaped through the portal as well. He shrugged, took a deep breath, squeezed his eyes shut, and stepped through.

Dru's bell-like laughter greeted him on the other side. "Open your eyes, Oriscoe. You look silly."

He did as she bid him, a trace of a smile on his lips. "Hey, I've never visited Hell before."

Dru sniffed. "We prefer 'Gehenna.'"

"Sure, I can see that."

"You know, the Christians mucked it all up. There's no fire and brimstone at all. That's why Mommy's portals look that way. It's a joke."

"Yes, a hilarious one, too," said Liz with a grin.

They stood in a room constructed entirely from obsidian, but bright, modern lights filled the space with warm yellow light. A thick Persian carpet covered the black stone floor, and an ornate ebony door closed off the room. The aged bronzed hardware on the door was Georgian style. A double of the portal in Dru's apartment flickered and danced behind them, casting more reds and oranges on the polished black stone.

Leery whistled low and long. "Nice place, Princess."

Dru flashed a lopsided smile at him and nodded once. "Here, I won't correct you. Mommy's a stickler for the old forms."

"Good to know."

"When we come into her presence, you may meet her gaze when you greet her, but don't stare, and don't hold her gaze too long," Dru said to Liz. "Since you are witch, she will consider you one of her subjects."

Leery glanced at Liz, who nodded, solemn-eyed.

"And you," said Dru, turning to Leery. "Try not to be too forward. Her aura will call to you, there's no doubt. She can turn it off about as much as you can resist free coffee. Try to keep it in your pants. Daddy can be jealous inside the palace."

"Uh, right. Should I stay here?"

"No!" Dru beamed at him. "She wants to meet you, and I want you to meet her. Daddy, too, if he's around." She turned and walked to the door, and as she did, Liz chucked Leery in the ribs again.

"What?" he mouthed.

Liz shook her head sadly and followed Drusilla bat Agrat into the halls of her mother's home.

9

After what seemed like miles and miles of obsidian corridors, Dru led them to a pair of doors. The thick slabs stretched from the floor to the ceiling, which was lost in shadows one hundred yards above their heads. Each door was as wide as three big men standing shoulder to shoulder and looked as though they might weigh as much as a compact car. Dru turned the knob of the door on the right and flung it open without apparent effort. "Mommy! Are you in here?" she called.

The voice that answered her boomed like thunder, but at the same time, seemed to caress Leery like a lover. "Drusilla! Baby, you come right over here and let me look at you!"

Dru glanced over her shoulder and dimpled at Leery. "Mommy, I've brought friends. Could you cover yourself? My partner might explode if you don't."

"Oh, my!"

The sultry tone made Leery's blood race, his pulse pound, and his breathing accelerate.

"Down boy," mouthed Dru, a twinkle in her eye.

"Bring them before me," said Agrat.

Dru turned back to her mother and nodded. "Thanks, Mommy." She waved for Liz and Leery to follow and stepped inside the room. "Mommy, may I present my partner, Lerome Oriscoe, and our Magical Examiner, Elizabeth Hendrix." She bowed her head and waved her hand to her side. She turned and looked at Leery. "Leery, Liz, allow me to present her August Majesty, Agrat bat Mahlat, Sovereign of Demons, Commander of the Eighteen Legions, Queen of the Shabbat, Angel of Divine and Sacred Prostitution, Wife to Hercule, Dancing Roof-Demon, Mistress of Sorcery, One of the Four Queens of Gehenna, She of the Great and Terrible Name, and my mother."

"Close your mouth, Leery," Liz whispered.

Agrat bat Mahlat sat on an ornate throne carved from onyx and chased with garnet. She crooked one knee over the arm of her throne, her other calf hooked on her ankle. She wore a black silk robe. Her long hair was as black as midnight on a new moon, and her eyes glowed a deep red that recalled butchery and blood. A marvelous set of horns rose from her forehead and swept back over her head before curving toward the ceiling. Her lips glistened a bright, arterial red, as though they'd interrupted her sucking the blood from a virgin.

In other words, she looked a lot like Dru.

Leery stood and stared, while Liz dropped to one knee, head bowed. He tried to look away but couldn't quite pull his gaze from her beautiful face.

A coquettish smile lounged on her lips much the same way as she lounged in her chair. Her gaze caressed Leery, traversing his body with frank appreciation. "Have you taken him, dear one? He's cute."

"Mommy! He's my partner!"

Agrat tilted her head to the side in a rapid flick. "His attraction for you is plain, baby girl. I mean, look at my appearance. Look at how he sees me."

"Mommy, it's not polite to point these things out. He can control it no more than you."

She shrugged. "And this is the Magical Examiner? The one I've heard so much about?" Her gaze traveled to Liz.

Hendrix preened under her gaze, blushing, yet smiling. "Your Majesty."

Agrat's gaze flicked to the body bag hanging loose in Leery's grip. "And what have you brought me?"

"Mommy, we've run into something we need your help with." Dru glanced at Leery and motioned for him to put the body down. Liz ran back the zipper.

"Your Majesty," said Liz. "I discovered the residue of a form of magic I'm unfamiliar with."

"Kabbalah," Leery croaked.

Agrat glanced at him and smiled. She sniffed the air. "Yes, I believe the cute one is right. This is the sorcery I passed to the Lost Tribes. But it's different...*marked*..." She squinted and came off her throne with the fluid grace of a ballerina. She strutted closer, her eyes smoldering. She knelt next to the body and bent over the gaping neck wound. Her tongue extended delicately, then snapped out, quick as a snake, and lapped at the rent flesh. "This tastes of a wolf, as well as Kabbalah. It is *aumrecht zayt* magic. This was worked by one open to darkness, to perversion. It smells of corruption, of a *toyt eyner*."

Liz glanced at Leery.

"It's black magic." He nodded at Agrat. "Magic of the 'other side.' It smells of a zombie."

"Zombies and werewolves. But it is *your* magic?" asked Dru.

"It sprouted from what I taught," said Agrat. "But it is no more mine than is the so-called *rekhte zeyt* magic. I make no such distinctions. I taught Amemar the basics, how to sense and manipulate the underpinning energies of all things. What he did with it is his own."

"Cuh..." Leery cleared his throat, blushing. "Can you tell us who cast it?"

"I am unable to do so."

Dru's eyes narrowed. "But you *can*?"

Agrat turned her gaze on her daughter's, serenity radiating from her face. "I am unable to do so," she repeated.

"Is it Uncle Luci?" asked Dru in a quiet voice.

"Dear, don't press me. And don't go running to your uncle. He's busy this time of year, and he's not involved at any rate."

"Then who? Aunt Lily? Auntie Naamah? Auntie Eisheth?"

"Sweet one, do not trouble your aunts. Besides, Lillith no more cares for the machinations of the dead than do I." She turned her gaze on Leery again. "We much prefer men with a pulse." The raw sexuality in her voice drew Leery a step forward.

"Mother!" hissed Dru.

"If you're not going to mark him, dearest, do not object if others wish to invite him to play."

"Agrat!" snapped a man's cold voice. "Do not tease our daughter!"

Dru's head snapped around, and Leery followed her gaze. "Daddy!" She turned and dashed to the regal-looking man standing in the open doorway.

His skin was pale, pale, pale, and his bone-white hair lay slicked back over his head. His eyes had faded to a soft pink. He wore a midnight-blue silk suit with a blood-red cravat. Blue veins laced his delicate hands, and long age-yellowed nails tipped his slender fingers. His gaze traveled to Dru, then snapped to Leery's face and narrowed. He darted a glance at his wife, then returned to Leery's face. "We shall speak, sir, before you leave this place."

"Oh, Daddy," sighed Dru. She stepped closer to him and threw her arms around his neck. "This is my friend, Lerome Orsicoe."

"Call me, Leery, Your Majesty."

"Indeed," Hercule murmured. "And we shall speak."

"Oh, Daddy. Leave him be."

"No, dearest girl. I shall know his intentions ere he leaves this hall."

Dru sighed and hugged his neck again. "I've missed you, Daddy. Mommy, too."

"You may always return home, dearest Drusilla. We've kept your room just so."

"They have come for my help, Husband," said Agrat. "They've brought evidence of a most particular spell."

"Indeed?" His cold, dead gaze left those of his daughter, flitted to Agrat's, and once again settled on Leery. His nostrils flared. "And a wolf, to boot," he murmured.

"Oh, Daddy," sighed Dru as she nestled against his chest. "Don't be a bigot."

"Come and see," said Agrat. "Tell us what you can see of this magic."

Smiling down at her, Hercule disengaged from Dru's embrace and walked to the corpse. He paused and looked down at Liz Hendrix, who still knelt on one knee. She peeked at him and shuffled back a step. His gaze traveled to the side of her neck, hovering over her carotid artery. "No, child. You have nothing to fear from me. Even if Agrat would allow me to harm one of her subjects—which I assure you, she would not—you are our guest, and I would no more allow you to come to harm as I would my own daughter. Besides, I'm well fed." He smiled, which unfortunately showed off his impressive fangs and did nothing to assuage Liz's discomfort.

Then, he glared down at Kay Soper's remains and sniffed. "One of the lowest caste," he said. "She shall rise soon."

"Wait a minute. A vampire?"

Hercule broke into scornful laughter. "No, *wolf*. I said one of the lowest caste. I believe they are called zombies in modern parlance."

"Ah. That makes sense," said Leery. Since Hercule had arrived, Agrat had turned down the wattage, and blood was once again flowing to his brain.

"*This* makes sense to you?" asked Hercule, sweeping his hand to encompass Soper's corpse.

"He means the part about Soper turning zombie, Daddy. We recently had a run-in with the Zombie mafia."

"God's bones, Drusilla!" snapped Hercule. "You must resign this insane profession and return home this very day!"

"Oh, Daddy," sighed Dru. "Let's not argue this again."

Hercule's gaze snapped to Leery. "You will protect her!"

"Of course, I will, but I have to tell you, Sire, she needs very little protection."

Hercule harrumphed and turned his gaze to Agrat. "Can you not speak sense to her?"

"Love, she is her own woman."

"Woman? She's barely born!"

"Hercule, Hercule," said Agrat with tender sympathy. "Our daughter is a succubus of royal birth, a vampire in her own right, and a woman of the police. One almost dares not stand in the same room with her."

"*Mais c'est de la folie! Notre enfant ne doit pas se mettre en danger pour sa passion! Nous devons la protéger, garder le monde à distance, garder les loups comme ça, ça, cet homme de sa porte!*"

"Oh, Daddy," said Dru with fondness in her voice. "I'll be fine. And this wolf is a fine man. In your day, he would have been a knight atop a grand horse, wearing a suit of armor. You'd find him standing between the innocent and the terrors of the world. Just as you would do for me."

"Hercule, she has grown, love."

Dru's father turned a squinting gaze on Leery and looked him up and down. "*Si tu es blessée, ma chère fille, je le tiendrai responsable.*"

"Daddy!" Dru stamped her foot. "You are not listening to me. If I am hurt, I don't hesitate to say my body will fall *on top of* Leery's. *Tu comprends, Papa? Ce loup que vous méprisez mourrait avant qu'il ne me permette de faire du mal. Je sais cela.*"

"*Je comprends que vous croyez que cela est vrai, ma chère, mais le pense-t-il?*"

"Yeah, he does. Dru is correct. I *would* die before I allowed her to come to harm." said Leery. The room fell silent, and all eyes turned to him. "Hey, I needed a foreign language in high school, and all the pretty girls took French."

"Make no jokes, wolf!" snapped Hercule.

"Who said I was joking? I'm telling you, Hercule, if you think I'd let something happen to Dru that I could prevent, you're a beer short of a six-pack."

Hercule's eyes narrowed even farther, until a mere hint of pink could be seen through his long white lashes. "I hold you responsible! I have heard your oath!" His eyes blazed wide, and his chin came up so he could glare down his nose at Oriscoe.

"Fine by me, chum," said Leery. "The name's Leery Oriscoe if you need to look me up."

"Daddy! Stop it!" Dru moved over to stand next to Leery. "You don't need his oath. I already told you how it would be." She stamped one dainty foot. "Now, stop this posturing and silliness! Leery is *also* your guest."

Some of the fire went out of Hercule's gaze, and his expression softened a notch. "Yes, well. *Vous devez pardonner à un vieil homme sa défense passionnée de sa fille et les bigoteries d'une époque révolue.*"

"*Ce n'est pas un problème.* Your daughter is a lovely person, and I don't begrudge you wanting to protect her." Leery nodded. "I have daughters of my own."

"Then you understand."

"Yes, I do."

"*C'est bon.*"

"There, you see, Daddy? I'm a good judge of character." Dru put her hand on Leery's arm, wrapping her fingers around the inside of his forearm. "Leery's one of the good ones."

Hercule nodded. "*Je connais tes intentions,*" he said, meeting Leery's gaze.

"My intentions, Your Majesty, are to be a good partner for your daughter. To keep her safe, even while she's keeping me safe. I haven't considered anything else."

"*C'est bon,*" Hercule said with a nod.

Agrat's eyes sparkled, and she wrinkled her nose at Dru.

"Now that we've got all that out of the way," said Dru, without meeting her mother's gaze, "what do you think of the magic, Daddy?"

"Yes. It is peculiar." His gaze darted to his wife's. "I take it your mother would not speak?"

"Was *unable* to speak," corrected Agrat.

"*Vous ne pouviez pas parler, oui.* She was unable to speak because of the undead element to the spell-crafting."

"Yes, the zees, right?"

"No. My wife would not hesitate to speak against such base beings. My wife was unable to speak because of her loyalty to me. You see, I know the person responsible for this spell."

"Who is it, Daddy."

Hercule grimaced. "It is one of mine, *ma chère. Pire encore,* you know him. *C'est* Pierre."

Dru's grip tightened on Leery's arm. "Oh, no, Daddy! It can't be!"

"*Mais oui, ma fille. Je ne te mentirais pas.*"

"Okay, let the peasant folk in on the joke. Who is Pierre?"

"Pierre Le Moyne de Châteauguay," said Hercule. "My friend of five centuries. Drusilla's godfather. And a vampire of my making."

"Oh..." Leery darted a glance at Dru, but she was looking at her shoes. "Uh..."

"Wait a second," said Liz. "Why would a Frenchman be versed in Kabbalic magic? *Rekhte zeyt* or *aumrecht zayt*?"

"The land of my birth had several...unfortunate incidents with the Jews," said Hercule.

Leery scoffed. "Ha. If that's what you want to call nearly a century of blood libel, torture and more deaths during the Inquisition, exiles, expulsions—"

"Yes, yes!" snapped Hercule. "The point is that Pierre's family purchased a title to avoid persecution. Their heritage was something of an open secret for a time. Their beliefs and their practices remained alive—at least during Pierre's natural life."

"Yes," said Agrat, gliding forward and inserting her hand into the crook of Hercule's arm. "Pierre is a Jew. He hides it, even now, but having lived through the time of blood libel after the First Crusade, I can't say I blame him."

"And he practices Kabbalah?" asked Liz.

Agrat gave a regal nod. "He is a Kabbalist, yes."

"I can't believe he would do this," murmured Dru.

"Nor I," said Hercule, lifting an eyebrow in his wife's direction.

"The spellcrafting belongs to Pierre. It's undeniable," Agrat said. "Though I can't say if he was coerced or not. He did not *cast* the spell, however."

"We can find out easy enough." Dru turned and began padding toward the door. "Don't tell him I'm coming, Daddy," she said over her shoulder.

"Uh, I need to take this back with me if she's about to rise," said Liz as she closed the oversized zipper of Kay Soper's body bag.

Hercule started after Dru, but Agrat held him fast. She smiled at Liz. "You may leave us. Mr. Oriscoe will bring the zombie-to-be."

"Uh... Yes, Your Majesty. Can I just say how delightful it was to meet you?"

Agrat smiled. "You may return. Just ask Drusilla."

"Thank you, Your Majesty!"

Agrat waved a languid hand, and Liz backed away, then turned and followed Dru.

Leery bent to retrieve the body. "Ah, grunt work. I guess I'd better—"

"You will wait," said Agrat. She watched until Liz passed out of hearing range, then turned an intense gaze on Leery. "My daughter has not marked you. Indeed, none of my kind have, though I see the marks of...*casual*...interactions all around you."

Leery cleared his throat. "In the course of my work—"

"Let us not be coy," said Hercule with an air of infinite weariness that only old vampires seemed able to pull off.

Leery shrugged. "Hey, what's wrong with a little fun between consenting adults?"

"Why, nothing," said Agrat. She dropped her hand from Hercule's arm and stepped close to Leery. "My husband is concerned about our daughter's physical safety. I—"

"Sure, I understand that. Like I said, I have daughters myself."

Agrat sniffed.

"It is not considered wise to interrupt one of the Four Queens of Gehenna," said Hercule from behind a lopsided smile.

"I apologize, Your Majesties. I'm a bit nervous."

Agrat flashed a grin at him, and in it, he thought he saw the suffering of the damned. "As I was saying... Hercule is concerned with our daughter's physical well-being, but I am concerned with *all* of Drusilla. Do you understand me, Mr. Oriscoe? Her physical, emotional, and mental well-being. Happiness is no less than she deserves, *n'est-ce pas*?"

Leery waited a moment, to be sure she had finished. "Yes, Your Majesty."

"My husband asked about your intentions. I do not. Intentions change with the winds. I have said none of my kind has marked you, in part due to Drusilla's handiwork. All of my kind can recognize her Royal touch." She reached out and tapped the amulet he wore under his shirt. The charm Dru had crafted for him. "But she can't stop me from marking you, Mr. Oriscoe."

Leery's gaze darted from Agrat's face to Hercule's, but the vampire's face may as well have been carved from pure white marble. "Uh, thanks, Your Majesty, but I..."

Agrat threw back her head and laughed—full-throated, belly-shaking laughter. Leery grinned a little, but Hercule only stared. Leery recognized the expression on his face; he'd used it on his own daughter's boyfriends after all.

"Cute *and* funny," said Agrat. "But no, Mr. Oriscoe, I am not marking you for myself. Rather, I mark you for Drusilla." She shrugged with her eyebrows. "Somewhere during her formative years, she developed queer ideas about morality, and she seems recalcitrant to take this step herself."

"Your Majesties, I think you have the wrong idea here. Dru and I are not—"

"She may never draw you close, Mr. Oriscoe. As I said, she has peculiar notions about what is proper. But your flirtations with others of my kind are at an end, even if she doesn't. I can't allow you to continue consorting with my kind. It may hurt my daughter if you do."

"Hurt..." Leery dropped his gaze, and when he lifted it, he first met Hercule's, then Agrat's. "I have never encouraged—"

"Shh," said Hercule.

"Yes, shh," repeated Agrat. "I, too, will hold you responsible if Drusilla is injured, same as Hercule. But..." She sidled closer, narrowing her eyes. "I will also hold you responsible for any emotional hurts you cause her. Do you understand?"

Leery swallowed hard. "I don't want Dru hurt, either. But I can't control everything that might happen. I will say that if she's hurt when we are together, it will be because I am unable to take that hurt in her place."

"And the rest?" asked Agrat.

"I have no intention of—"

"We've spoken about that."

"Mr. Oriscoe," said Hercule. "Are you familiar with the phrase, 'Hell hath no fury like a woman scorned?'"

"Sure, Your Highness. Everyone is, I imagine."

"In the original form, the idiom went like this, 'Hell hath no fury like the Witch Queen scorned.'" He lay his hand on his wife's shoulder. "It is about Agrat, *n'est-ce pas*? And even Luci walks with care when my wife is angry."

Leery held up his hands in supplication. "Your daughter is wonderful: beautiful, smart, funny—"

"Sexy," said Agrat.

"—and one of the few truly good people I've met, but she's my partner, and some things I don't mix."

Agrat sniffed. "Are you sure Drusilla will leave the choice up to you?"

"If you think she wouldn't, you don't know her as well as you think you do."

Hercule rocked forward on the balls of his feet, eyes snapping fire, and opened his mouth to lay into Leery, but Agrat put her hand on his arm.

"No, Hercule," she said. "He understands his responsibilities, and that's all we wanted." She dimpled at her husband, reminding Leery so much of Dru that his heart ached for a moment. "Besides, he is right about her in all respects." She nodded to Leery, and, taking her husband by the hand, she turned and left the room.

Leery watched them go, then sighed and bent to retrieve Kay Soper's remains.

IO

Leery found Liz and Dru waiting for him outside the room containing the portal back to the Locus of New York. They chatted pleasantly as he approached, the conversation punctuated with Dru's bell-like laughter and Liz's heartier chuckle.

"Joe's Pizza," he called. "You ladies order a corpse-eroni?"

"Cute," said Liz.

"Or something," said Dru.

"Right, right." Leery came alongside them and pointed at the door with Soper's feet. "One of you two comedy critics want to get that door for me?"

"We were just discussing that. We need to go see Pierre," said Dru.

"But I need to get back. Can you drop the remains by when you're finished?" asked Liz.

"Of course, we can," said Dru.

"Not for nothing, but I don't really want to go traipsing around down here with a corpse that may be revivifying."

"We could leave her here," said Dru with a shrug. "Mommy and Daddy wouldn't mind too much."

"Maybe your side of the portal would be better. In case she wakes up," said Liz. "You could lock her in the bathroom or something."

Dru nodded. "I've got just the place." She opened the door and walked to the portal, then disappeared through it.

Leery glanced at Liz. "Ladies first."

"Such chivalry." Her face twisted in a wry smile as though she understood perfectly what had gone on between Leery and Dru's parents.

Together, they followed Dru through the portal, where Liz said goodbye, and Leery put Kay Soper's remains in a small, tiled square room in the back of the pantry. The chamber had a door that locked from the outside and a drain set in the center of the floor. Dru threw the locks and turned back toward the hall leading to the portal.

"Wine cellar?" Leery asked.

"Uh, something like that."

"What?" Leery cupped his ear. "I didn't quite hear that, but, nah, it doesn't look like a serial killer's murder room at all, Dru."

"Very funny." She stopped at the mouth of the hall and turned to face him. "What did Mommy and Daddy want?"

"Oh, that? That was nothing. Stock tips."

"Stock tips?" Dru arched an eyebrow.

"Sure. I can really pick 'em."

"I'll...uh...keep that in mind." She turned as if to walk down the hall but didn't move. "Sorry about my parents, Leery. Daddy gets so—"

"Hey, you should've seen me on my daughters' prom nights. Talk about scary."

Dru chuckled. "I'll bet. Did you do that thing you do in the interview room?"

"What thing?"

"You know, where you buddy up to them and drop the ax when they start to warm up."

"Well, sure. That's just good meet-my-new-boyfriend behavior. How do you think I learned to do it?"

"And Mommy... She can be—"

"Dru, it's fine. They love you and want you protected. That's all that was. No harm, no foul."

"Just don't..." She shook her head.

"Come on, Dru. You can say anything to me. We're partners, remember?"

"Just don't date my mother. Okay?"

"Nothing to worry about there. I've sworn off your mother's kind."

For a moment, Dru's spine stiffened, but then she laughed. "Sure, you have, Leery. I bet you have a date with either Deli or Ella tonight. Oh, God...not *both*?"

"Nope. I had a pleasant evening planned: standing in some bushes and getting infested by ticks."

"Oh, now that sounds like fun."

"Hey, Nogan, don't knock it until you try it."

"Come on, Snoopy."

"What, I only looked in one or two of your drawers."

Dru shook her head and darted a flirty glance over her shoulder. "Did you like what you saw?"

Leery cleared his throat. "So, uh, this guy...this Pierre. You've...uh...known him long?"

"He's my *godfather*, Leery, so yeah, you could say I've known him my whole life."

"Right, right. And he's a vampire, too?"

Dru nodded, her long sable hair bouncing fetchingly as she opened the door to the portal room. "Yes. Daddy made him in the fifteenth century. Some kind of deal with the Le Moyne family back in France."

"Uh-huh."

"Daddy used to make a lot of vampires back then. It was before the Unification of the Covenants, and before he met Mother. Back then, he sort of needed an army."

"With the War of Fangs raging, I'll bet he did."

Dru cringed a little without turning. "Yeah. Sorry about all that 'wolf' business. The fighting got pretty bitter, I guess. He won't ever talk about it, but Mommy told me a few things. Some of the Packs turned brutal, savage."

"Hey, we're *wolves*. Besides, the way I heard it, your father's folk gave as good as they got."

"Probably," she said with a shrug. "But the war went on and on for hundreds of years. Plenty of time to learn to hate the enemy."

"I get it."

"Come on, let's go see Pierre." She stepped through the portal.

"Hopefully, Pierre's gotten past his hatred of wolves," muttered Leery. "Getting braced by two Old Fangs in one morning could get old."

He followed Dru through into Agrat bat Mahlat's obsidian palace, then followed her outside its walls. Her family digs sat atop a steep hill, like a scarab perched on a corpse's nose. The valley stretched away beneath them, filled with arid greens and even an anemic babbling brook cut through its center. The sky was like burnished bronze, though a little hazy with orange flashes he could only see from the tails of his eyes.

The hills defining the valley were capped with palaces similar to the one Dru grew up in, done in various stones, though all were dark and foreboding. Smaller structures descended the hills, but the floor of the valley was left clear—like a grand park.

"Wow," Leery said. "Who knew Hell was this nice?"

"Gehenna, Leery," said Dru.

"Oh, right. Gehenna. What's the property value like?"

Dru looked at him askance, a wry grin crinkling her face. "You wouldn't want to pay the price, Oriscoe. Trust me."

"So you're filthy rich? Is that what you're telling me?"

Dru rolled her eyes. "Come on, Goofy."

"You're really embracing this dog thing, Nogan."

"Sure am." Her bell-like laughter rang out and echoed across the otherwise silent valley.

"Who owns all those big places up at the top?"

Dru pointed at the closest one. "Aunt Lily." She flickered her finger down the line on the left side. "Auntie Naamah." Her finger pointed across the valley. "Auntie Eisheth. She and Naamah don't get on all that well, which means Lilith and she don't get on. Mommy's kind of caught in the middle."

"And that big place at the other end?"

"Uncle Luci's."

Leery turned his gaze toward the craggy, dull black stone edifice. "Are those carvings?"

"Bas relief. The 'miseries of Hell' and all that."

"Then, it's all just a big joke?"

"Well... Let's just say it's best to keep on Uncle Luci's good side."

"I can get down with that. Remind me if I start getting carried away when I meet him."

"Will do."

"Does good ole Pierre live in one of those big jobs at the top?"

"Oh, Pierre doesn't live here."

"Uh...okay. Then do you mind telling me what we're doing back here in Huh— In Gehenna?"

"Nice save. We're here because travel is easier here than on our side. We'll just pop over to the Portal Authority."

"The Portal Authority? You're kidding."

Dru shook her head. "It's that granite building near the valley floor." She pointed at a squat rectangular building next to the brook.

"Where does he live? France?"

"Don't be silly, Leery. He has a mansion in Los Angeles."

Leery chuckled. "A fifteenth-century vampire chose LA over all the other places in the world to live?"

"And all the other realms." Dru flashed a smile and nodded at him. "Pierre loves movies. Especially—"

"Don't tell me! I'm getting a vision... 'Interview With The Vampire' starring Brad Pitt and Tom Cruise?"

"No, he *hated* that one. He goes in for romantic comedies."

"Huh. My visions are usually right... Are you sure he doesn't only pretend to hate Lestat?"

They reached the Portal Authority, and Dru swept inside like she owned the place. "Two for Los Angeles," she said. "The residence of Pierre Le Moyne de Châteauguay."

"Right away, Your Grace," said the gray-skinned little man behind the counter. He clacked away at a computer terminal. "Right this way, Princess." He stepped from behind the counter and bowed to Dru, then cast a disapproving gaze at Leery. He led them to a circle of shimmering blue-white light standing on end. "Your portal, Your Highness. Please tell your mother I was happy to serve."

"Yes," said Dru, waving her hand back toward the entry. "Come on, Leery." She stepped into the flickering light and disappeared.

With a shrug, Leery followed her, reappearing a moment later in the middle of Mapleton Drive. Dru had already moved to the narrow swatch of grass in front of him, and he stepped to her side, his eyes roving across the massive faux-French chateau. "Your godfather goes in for understatement, eh?"

Dru chuckled and slapped at his arm. "Yeah, sure. Come on, I'll introduce you to Pierre."

"Are you sure we don't need backup, Dru?"

She stopped and cocked her head as though the thought had never occurred to her. "Oh, Pierre could never do anything to hurt me, and I'll make sure he doesn't do anything to hurt you, either." She walked to the drive and then up to the gate. She leaned down and pressed the call button, then grinned up at the camera. Dru gave a cutesy little wave when the gates trundled open. "Follow my lead with him, Leery," she whispered.

Leery shrugged and mimicked her silly wave at the camera. "I'm not sure I can pull that off, Nogan. I'm not quite as cute as you."

Dru flashed her dimples at him, then turned and walked across the oval-shaped drive to the arc-studded entrance. A short, foppish man stood next to the grand doors that led inside the vast place.

"*Ma chérie!*" he called in a high-pitched voice. "You haven't come to see me in so long, *mon amour!*"

"I'm sorry, Pierre. My new job has kept me so busy."

Pierre's gaze flicked to Leery but never made it up to his face. He wore a blue velvet coat that fell to mid-thigh and a matching vest with gold stars embroidered every inch or so. A golden watch chain stretched from the second button from the top to his watch pocket. His gray tweed pants covered the tops of shoes polished to a mirror gloss. His skin was pasty-pale, and his eyes seemed to match the light-blue of faded denim. His black hair was shaved on the sides but long on top and swept back over the crown of his head with some kind of hair treatment. He wore a substantial handle-bar mustache over his pale pink lips. He bent at the waist and leaned close to Dru. "Who is this man?" he faux whispered.

"Leery Oriscoe," said Leery, holding out a hand.

"He's my partner, Pierre."

"Indeed?" His nostrils flared, and his mustache twitched. "And your father approves?"

"They've met," said Dru with a one-shouldered shrug.

"A wolf, no?" Again, his gaze darted toward Leery without making eye-contact. "This is most—"

"He's my *partner*, Pierre...on the police force."

Pierre tittered and fanned his face. "*Mon Dieu, ma chérie!* You gave me such a fright." He chuckled with relief while looking anywhere but at Leery. He flapped his hands at his sides. "Where are my manners? Come in! Come in!" He backed inside and swept his hand to encompass the aircraft-hangar-sized foyer.

Leery followed Dru inside, noting the black-out curtains pulled closed over the tall windows ringing the room. He stopped a few paces from the open door, then stepped back and pulled it shut. Pierre flashed him what he guessed was the same fake smile he used on his servants.

Dru walked to the center of the space and spun in a slow circle, her gaze darting here and there. "I love what you've done this time,

Pierre. You must give me your designer's name."

"An old man must keep some secrets from the younger generations."

"You're not old, Pierre."

"Alas, I am. I am. And I know it. These times are..." He shook his head. "Hercule has it so easy down there with your mother. None of the pressures of the modern age to contend with."

"Just the pressures of living with Mother," said Dru with a grin.

"Such cheek!" laughed Pierre, humor glinting in his eyes. "But tell me, Princess, is this a social visit?"

"Can we go to your library, Pierre? I love the furniture in there."

"But, of course, *ma chérie!*" He cast a corner-of-the-eye glare at Leery. "Will your friend come, too, or will he await us here?"

His tone made it clear he'd prefer Leery to stand there in the foyer until the universe wound down, but Dru only laughed. "You're so funny, Pierre." As she turned toward a set of doors leading deeper into the house, she threw a surreptitious wave for Leery to follow. Pierre sniffed but didn't object as Oriscoe fell into step with them.

Dru led them to a room paneled in cherry and lined with floor-to-ceiling bookshelves crammed tight with hard-bound books of every color and material. A Persian rug covered a perfect square in the center of all those books, and on it rested two chaise lounges and four wing-backed chairs, all upholstered in blue suede. Without waiting to be invited, Dru crossed to one of the wing-backed chairs and sank into it. She patted the chair next to her and tossed her hair at Leery. Pierre moved to her other side and sank to the edge of one of the lounges.

"Tell me, Princess. To what do I owe this honor?"

"I think you know, Pierre," said Dru in a soft voice.

Pierre cocked his head to the side and glanced between Dru and Leery. "I'm sure I don't."

"We have a case back in the Locus of New York. A murder case."

Pierre lifted both hands, leaned back in his chair, then spread his arms as though to say, "This is Los Angeles."

"He's cute, Dru," grunted Leery.

Pierre narrowed his eyes and hissed.

"Whoa, settle down there, sparky."

"Both of you cut it out right this instant!" Dru snapped. "Pierre, the case is strange, and Daddy said you might be able to help us out. He said you have a certain proficiency in the kind of magic we found residue for on the body."

"Oh?" Pierre's face turned cold and hard as he stared at Leery. "*Et qu'est-ce que votre père pense de cet animal?*"

"*Il a également pensé 'cet animal' ne pouvait pas parler français,*" said Leery with a sour grin.

"We visited him first. Now, we are here." She cocked her head to the side. "What does that tell you? And, yes, he was also surprised 'the animal' could speak French. Arrogance is ugly, Pierre."

Pierre dropped his gaze to the floor between them. "Yes. Well, old habits..."

"This 'animal' wasn't even born when you idiots fought the War of Fangs."

"Yes," repeated Pierre.

"You haven't asked about the magic." Dru scooted forward to sit on the edge of her chair, staring at Pierre with hard eyes. "I wonder why?"

Pierre started and looked her in the eye. "What kind of magic? I'm not much of a magician."

"But you *are* a Kabbalist," said Leery. "I can smell it on you."

Pierre grunted. *"Redt 'der khih' aoykh eydish?"*

"Yo," said Leery with a shrug. "I speak Yiddish—and Hebrew to save you from asking."

"Will wonders never cease?" murmured Pierre. "So. You found a woman murdered, find evidence of *aumrecht zayt* magic, and your father sends you to me?" He shook his head. "I should be angry with Hercule."

"First, we never said it was a woman. Second, we never mentioned *aumrecht zayt*," said Leery.

"No, Princess Drusilla said you had a case of a murdered woman in the Locus of New York. And of course, any Kabbalic magic used in a murder would be *aumrecht zayt*."

"No, Pierre," said Dru in a soft voice. "I never said the victim was a woman."

"And we never said the magical residue was involved in the murder."

Pierre froze where he sat—only his gaze moved, flicking back and forth between Dru and Leery.

"Pierre, you need to talk to us," said Dru.

"You have no jurisdiction here, and you are not here in an official capacity, or Los Angeles policemen would have come with you."

"All that's true, Pierre."

"But we can change that. Dru can stay here—you know, in case you get the urge to lace up your boogie shoes—while I go get everything officialized."

The air whoofed out of Pierre, and he slumped against the lounge's cushioned back. "I..." He shook his head. "They didn't give me a choice." His white face flushed to pale gray. "I...*owe* certain people."

"The Zombie mafia?"

"Yes, Princess." He twitched his hands at the room around them. "This place is expensive, and I made a string of poor choices..."

Dru heaved a sigh. "Daddy would have helped you."

Pierre placed a hand over his eyes. "Of course, he would. He always does." He pursed his lips and scuffed away the trickle of blood dripping from the corner of his left eye. "I wanted to do this myself. I..."

"Tell us," said Leery. "All of it."

"They will stake me," he whispered.

"Not if you are with Mommy and Daddy in Gehenna."

Pierre's gaze swam about the room, lingering on the spines of certain books, on the paintings that dotted the walls where no bookshelves stood. "They will destroy my home."

"And what will happen if you are sent to a dungeon?" asked Leery.

Pierre sighed. "Aida Rocha."

"Cripes. The head of the LA branch of *Noster Est*? That Aida Rocha?"

Pierre nodded, misery scarring his features. "I owe her money. A lot of money."

"And you fell behind in the payments," whispered Dru.

"Yes. A zee horde came to visit. They..." He dropped his hand from his eyes, leaving the pink smear of bloody tears behind. "They offered me choices. Pay money I didn't have, create a spell, or enter indentured servitude with *Noster Est* for twenty-five years. My businesses"—his eyes scanned the room again—"my home, everything, would have come under their contract. I couldn't give it up." His gaze settled on Dru's. "Do you know the first time I saw respect returned in Hercule's gaze?"

Dru shook her head.

"When he visited me here. He said, 'You've done well on your own, Pierre.'"

"Yes," she whispered.

"I couldn't let him see me fail."

"Tell us about the spell," she said, dashing a hand across her eyes.

"Spells. Two spells with different targets— one generic, one specific." His voice firmed. "The first required a strange illusion that—"

"What kind of illusion?" asked Leery.

"They gave me a few photos. Photos of a werewolf. They wanted the attacker to appear as the wolf in the photographs."

"And what about the victims, Pierre?" asked Dru.

"Yes. The zees said women would be killed by the first spell's target, and that I was to bind their spirits to their body for a time. To provide a way back in, you see, in case they wanted the dead woman to join the ranks of *Noster Est*."

"To make a zombie, in other words."

"Yes, Mr. Oriscoe. To create one of the lowest caste of the undead."

"You said there were two spells. One generic, one specific?"

Pierre nodded. "They also wanted a spell to control a specific man—a Hassid. They said his faith was great, but that he had a vulnerability. This entrancement was to allow someone to call the Hassid and give him instructions—instructions that would be a compulsion, you understand. He would have no choice but to obey."

Dru's gaze cut to Leery's and then away. "Did they say who this Hassid is?"

"No," said Pierre. "I just crafted the incantations. Someone else was to cast them. I got the feeling the Hassid would cast the *doppelgäng* spell once under control."

"And what was the point of all this? What's it all for?"

"This, I don't know. There were...certain complications. They wanted the compulsion to persist, and as I said, they wanted the *option* to turn the victims, but I couldn't do this last part. I had to make it a blanket effect."

"Every victim of this *doppelgänger* will turn?" asked Leery.

"I'm afraid so, but the damn zees don't know that."

Leery shook his head. "I hope your debt is paid, at least."

Pierre hung his head. "Aida says to me, 'This is but a payment, fanger.' I'm still their servant."

Dru stood and walked to one of the shelves, her gaze on the spines of the books. "You've risked a lot more than the respect of my father, Pierre."

"Yes, and stupidly."

"Hey, don't feel bad. These zombies are bad actors. They've perfected the art of the double-cross."

Pierre leaped to his feet. "You don't understand! How could you? You are but a wolf!"

"Pardon me, pal. I was just trying to make you feel better."

"They are the *lowest* caste! Do you not see? I am a *vampire*! They are but *zombies*!"

"And I'm just an animal that speaks four languages. So what?"

"I understand, Pierre," said Dru. "Maybe there is a way…"

He turned to stare at her back with hope dancing in his eyes. "*Oui*?"

"*Peut être*, Pierre. Maybe."

"I will do it. Whatever it is!"

"Come back to Gehenna with us this very moment. Just say you are visiting. The zees can't touch you at Mommy and Daddy's. If we need you, we will call on you there."

"*Oui, ma chérie. Oui.*"

II

By the time Leery and Dru stepped out of Gehenna and into her apartment, it was going on late afternoon, and the sun shone through her floor-to-ceiling living room windows. They stood for a moment, side-by-side, not touching, just watching the spectacle.

"Now, that's a view," said Leery.

"Eh, it's not so bad."

"A view of a brick wall that isn't moldy is 'not so bad,' Dru. That view"—he pointed at the sun-gilded skyline—"is spectacular."

"I suppose."

"You think Pierre will stay put?"

"Yes. He's used to a certain...reliance on Mommy and Daddy."

He glanced at her from the tail of his eye. "Well, I guess I'd better return Kay Soper to the ME."

"Right," said Dru, but neither of them moved. She sighed and transferred her weight to one foot, brushing her shoulder against Leery's arm. "It is a spectacular view, isn't it?"

"Sure is." She began to turn her head, and Leery snapped his eyes back to the sunset. "Gorgeous."

"Hungry?" Dru asked. "I think I have food."

"That's okay, partner. I'll grab something later."

"Are you sure? I don't mind. It'll give me a reason to practice."

"Eating or cooking?"

Dru shrugged and chuckled.

"Maybe another time," said Leery. "Let's go get that body bag."

Dru turned and led him back through the kitchen. She stepped into the pantry and stopped. "Uh, Houston? We have a problem."

Leery came up behind her and snorted. "That's what you call a 'problem?' I call that a disaster."

The door to the tiled room lay askew on the floor, pieces of the metal locks lay scattered on the pantry floor. Shreds of black vinyl were all that remained of the body bag.

"I guess she woke up," said Leery.

"And I guess she got stronger while she was dead. That door was reinforced." Dru shook her head. "I'd better call this in."

"Right. I'll call Hendrix and give her the bad news."

"No, I'll do that. Use that nose of yours downstairs. See if you can pick up her scent."

"Good idea."

"You can leave your clothes here. No use shredding another set."

Leery froze for an instant, but Dru didn't turn to look at him. "Uh, right." He backed out of the pantry and retraced his steps into the living room. "Hey, you know what would be good? Another amulet that held that illusion you cast on me during the Williams-Costello thing."

"Now, why didn't I think of that?"

Dru's voice held an edge of laughter, and Leery looked up just in time to catch the amulet before it smacked into his chest. "Oh, nice. Thanks, Dru."

"I made you look like a soccer mom."

"Oh… Well, better than a werewolf, I guess."

"Not in my opinion," said Dru.

Blushing, Leery slipped the leather loop over his neck. The amulet—a piece of onyx with a red flaw in the middle of it—hung to his solar plexus like the other one she'd given him. The extra length allowed room for changing to his wolf without popping the cord.

The red at the center of the onyx caught his eye, and he took the stone between his fingers to get a better look. As he moved the stone, the shape of the flaw seemed to flutter. First, it looked like a half-closed eye, then a key, and then a crescent moon. "Neat," he said.

"Glad you like it." Dru picked up her phone and started dialing. "I'll meet you out front after I make the calls."

"Right." Leery dropped the amulet and finished shedding his clothes. He took a deep breath and let his wolf out, then drew a deep breath through his nose. The zombie's scent flashed in his mind like a neon lightning storm, drawing him toward the foyer, and he moved off at a brisk pace. As he passed it, he glanced at the mirror above Dru's table in the entry and grinned.

She hadn't made him look like a soccer mom at all. He looked like Adonis.

12

Leery stood in the elevator next to a little old lady from the floor below Dru's penthouse suite. She stood behind one of those wheeled carts for schlepping groceries back from the corner, both hands curled around the handle as if she thought Leery would try to steal it from her. Every now and again, she'd peek up at him from the corner of her eye. If he'd been in his human form, he'd have said something to reassure her, but wolf vocalizations tended to have the opposite effect, so he kept mum. When the doors opened on the ground floor, she almost sprinted out of the elevator car.

Pulling another massive breath in through his nose, Leery caught the zombie's scent again. He followed the scent trail, taking giant walking steps until he was out of sight, then breaking into a jog. She hadn't taken the direct route out the lobby doors and into the street but rather had gone through service corridors into the alley.

He glanced back—he was supposed to meet Dru out front—but the urge to give chase to his prey was too strong, and he chucked open the alley door and stepped out.

13

Dru hung up after telling Hendrix about the missing corpse, then dialed the precinct and got routed through to Van Helsing's office. "Hey, Lieu."

"Nogan. Making progress?"

"Yes, I think so. We have an informant from Los Angeles—"

"I hope no giant-sized airfare bill is forthcoming."

"Uh, no. We, uh, used family resources."

"*We*, huh? I guess my package found its way into the right hands."

"Yes," said Dru.

"Fine. Go on."

"Our LA informant has ties to the Zombie mafia in that locus. He was asked to craft a particular set of spells—one to control someone, and one to blur a person's identity, and to link the souls of the person's victims to their bodies."

Van Helsing made a sound that would have made sense if she'd had a tongue to click against her teeth. "More zombie soldiers. Oh, well. We'll arrest them, too, given time. At least, that explains Johnny's identification."

"Yes."

"Good, I'll start the paperwork to cancel Oriscoe's holiday. Tell him if you see him, yeah?"

"Sure thing, Lieu."

"Well, good. I'll let you go—"

"There's something else, Lieu." She took a breath and explained about Kay Soper's unique escape. "We're going to track her tonight. See if we can grab her up before she makes it to a *Noster Est* safehouse."

"Do more than see if you can, Nogan."

"Right, boss." The line went dead, and Dru hung up. She went to her bedroom and retrieved her battlestaff, pausing a minute to channel power into its blood garnet. On her way out, she fluffed her hair in the same mirror Leery had used to check out her illusion and left. She rode the elevator down alone, thinking of how Leery had stood up to her mother's advances, a small smile playing at the corners of her mouth. It was a big deal to resist a sacred prostitute in her own home. It usually took some strong motivation like— When the direction of her thoughts dawned on her, she straightened and banished them, setting her mouth into a grim line.

The elevator disgorged her in the marble-clad lobby, and she strode out into the early evening without so much as looking either direction. Leery was nowhere to be seen— which meant he was on the scent.

Leaning her staff against her shoulder, she put her index fingers in her mouth and whistled loud enough to earn glares from those passing by her.

14

L eery paused as the ear-splitting whistle reached him, then threw back his head and howled before sprinting along the scent trail left by the freshly-minted zombie. Her odor seemed permeated with something that set his nerves aflame. The aroma of decay starting in her dead flesh was there, but there was something over the top of it. Something...enthralling.

He sprinted down the alley and burst out onto a small side street, not even bothering to check for oncoming traffic—either pedestrian or vehicular. Soper had gone right, and Leery leaned into his turn, the talons of his feet digging into the asphalt for added leverage.

He poured on the speed, not even noticing the way his chest rumbled in an unconscious snarl.

15

Dru cocked her head as the howl echoed from behind the building. She turned and trotted to the corner, then turned again, heading toward the mouth of the alley she knew emptied into the street at the corner of her building. She smiled as she ran, thinking of Leery's face when she'd told him she made him look like a soccer mom.

At the mouth of the alley, she spotted the furrows made by his claws as he executed a full-speed turn out of the narrow passage and followed on in the direction he'd run. Another alley mouth yawned half a block on, and she slowed as something big moved in its shadows.

16

Leery became aware of the insidious rage that had crept into his blood, of the snarl that now oozed from his mouth and nostrils, of the salivation that dripped from his fanged maw. It had been an ugly twenty-four hours, and trailing one of the authors of his pain had spoken to his wolf.

He followed Soper's trail as it ducked into another alleyway and poured on all the speed he could muster, growling and snarling with abandon.

17

The thing in the alley snarled and growled as it moved in the shadows. Dru slowed, then stopped. Shaped like a werewolf, the dark figure was beginning to sound like one, too. "Leery?" she called.

The wolf stepped out of the alley and stood glaring at her, drool hanging from its open mouth, its tail straight out, ears flattened along its skull, a black woolen hat perched on its head.

Did Leery have his hat? she asked herself.

A low rumble started in the wolf's chest, and it grew and grew and grew into a ferocious growl that chilled Dru's blood. "Whoa, whoa, whoa, big guy. It's Dru."

The wolf's lips peeled back from its fangs, and its yellow eyes narrowed to slits. It took a single step forward and spread its long arms wide.

Dru took a step back. "What's gotten into you, Leery?" She lifted her hand and dashed a few runes in the air, lighting the gloaming with cerulean light. "Rein it in, big guy."

The wolf snarled and leaped, and Dru shouted a word of power as she completed the last rune. A bubble of sapphire encapsulated her, hardening as the wolf slammed into it, and taking on a geometric pattern akin to a cut jewel. The wolf howled in frustration but didn't flee.

"Come on, now," said Dru. "We're friends...partners... Maybe more than that?"

The wolf's lips twitched and spasmed, its mouth yawning wide. It circled her, looking for an opening in her shield.

18

He had her cornered, trapped within the construct she thought would protect her from his rage. Soper cowered inside her walls—walls he could easily rend with his strength, his talons, the *power* that flowed in his veins. He circled her, the scent of her fear intoxicating him, urging him to violence.

Leery reached high above his head, extending his claws as far as he could, stretching for the oncoming night, for the power of the moon, of the stars, of the darkness... He brought his hand down with all the force he could muster.

19

The wolf raked its claws across her bubble, the tips of its claws leaving streamers of azure sparks behind. The blue light gleamed in the creature's eyes and lit the underside of the black woolen hat's brim. Its ears twitched, reacting to some far-off sound, but the yellow eyes never left Dru's.

"Leery! Leery, you can fight this!" She drew in the air, forming runes in a sickly yellow ochre. "I don't want to fight you, Leery! I don't want to hurt you!" Dru completed the last of eight runes, sketched in haste, and began to connect them with the Star of Ishtar. "Come on, Leery. Run, if you can't control it. I won't chase you. I won't cast on you." As she worked the lines between the runes, yellow ochre darkened into red ochre.

The wolf's gaze dipped away from hers for a moment, captivated by the glowing runes, the shifting hue. Its anger rumbled in its chest like an idling dragster, rough and uneven. Its yellow-eyed glare snapped back to her face, and it threw back its head and howled.

Then the wolf pounced, and Dru screamed.

20

The cardboard shredded beneath Leery's claws, and Kay Soper shrieked from within the refrigerator crate. His growl blossomed into a snarl as he ripped the fridge box apart, angry that she thought such a simple ruse would fool him.

Soper cowered inside, kneeling on the wet, filth-covered bricks next to the dumpster. Her skin hadn't yet taken on the aspects of carrion, but the odor of corruption washed over Leery as he leaned toward her, snarling, showing his teeth.

Leery advanced on the newly-birthed zombie in stiff-legged steps, his lips curled back, his tail stiff behind him. He crouched, bringing his fangs closer to her huddled form, the skin above his nose wrinkling and twitching.

Mere inches away, Leery froze and turned off his growl. He cocked his head as a strange howl echoed down the narrow alley. He straightened a mite and turned his head toward the alley mouth.

When Dru's scream reached him, he bolted away at top speed.

21

The wolf slammed into her shield, lashing out with tooth and claw, sending a thousand glowing blue sparks shimmering into the oncoming night. The beast snarled and thrashed, ravaging the gem-like surface of her bubble, leaving gouges in it that didn't reach all the way through, but which weakened the field of power, nonetheless. Its savage, barbarous attacks reached a fever-pitch of maniac frenzy— slashing and snapping, kicking and biting, anything and everything the wolf could muster to try to tear down her wall of force.

"Leery! Leery! I don't want to do this!" Dru shrieked.

The wolf paused for a heartbeat, narrow-eyed gaze pinning her where she stood, then began its onslaught again.

Dru connected the last rune, the final point of Ishtar's Star, and a brilliant scarlet light burst from the figure's center, piercing the gathering darkness like a sharp blade through paper. A word in the *Verba Patiendi* danced on her tongue, yet she did not give it life. Her red-eyed gaze sought the wolf's yellow, her rune set pulsing with bloody, candy-apple-red vehemence.

The wolf snarled and slashed, growled and gouged at her shield—vicious, hateful, murderous. "Leery! I can't hold back! Not with you like this!"

The wolf howled at the sky, then continued to thrash at her shield, and Dru despaired.

22

L eery burst out of the shadowed alley and into the smoky dregs of dusk. He whirled to the right, his chartreuse eyes glowing like spotlights in the gloaming. Seeing nothing, he twisted to the left, his gaze zeroing in on the electric-blue flashes reflecting off the storefront at the next intersection. He leaped toward the corner, pouring on the speed.

He rounded the corner and stuttered a step or two, unable to credit his vision. Another wolf thrashed against a bubble of magical power that surrounded Dru. Another werewolf in a black wool hat. Another brown and gray furred wolf...

He shook his head and lifted his snout to catch the creature's scent on the wind, but the scent that reached him was impossible! It was his own scent. Snarling, Leery pistoned his legs, leaping the remaining distance to the bubble in a single bound, and came down swinging and snarling.

The other version of himself looked up from Dru's sphere as Leery reached them, and the fight was on. They both crashed to the ground, snarling and clawing and biting and tearing and rolling and kicking. Leery rent the flesh on the imposter's chest with a double-handed swipe of his talons. The imposter lashed out with his feet, raking Oriscoe's legs from his hips to his knees. Leery slammed forward, trying to bury his fangs in the imposter's throat, but the other wolf pinned his jaws to his chest, snarling and snapping at Leery's face.

They rolled back and forth across the two-lane asphalt, neither seeming able to get the upper hand and setting off what sounded like every dog on the block. Leery switched tactics, burying his fangs in one of the imposter's wrists and grabbing at his other arm with both fists. He slammed his weight forward on the other wolf, trying to hold him still, but it was like wrestling an eel.

A tingling, hot net of cherry-red witchcraft settled over them both, sizzling and snapping like a live wire, and its weight pressed them both into the macadam, unrelenting, uncaring. *Dru*, Leery thought with a wolfish grin. The spell began to drain him of strength, of power, and Leery felt the weakness overcoming his opponent.

"Leery?" asked Dru, her hands busy tracing runes of back-up spells in the night air. "Which one is you?"

The wolf beneath him yipped, and Leery snarled, letting go of the imposter's wrist and shaking his head.

"I can't tell which is which, even knowing about Pierre's spell." She stepped closer, peering down at them. "*I should be able to tell!*"

Leery shifted atop of the other wolf, keeping his weight bearing down, intent on draining the imposter that much quicker. He drew his legs up around the imposter's hips, sitting astride him like an MMA fighter in full mount, and put both hands on the other wolf's collar bones, pressing him down.

"Stop that!" Dru snapped.

Leery shook his head and whined.

"How am I to tell you apart?" Dru had two rune sets completed, just waiting on a word of power to ignite them. Both glowed a brilliant red—bright enough to read by at midnight.

There's only one thing to do, thought Leery. His wolf shook his head. *You know it's the only way. She can handle him now that he's as drained as we are.* A low rumble came from his own chest, but it tapered to a whine, and Leery changed back to his human form.

The wolf beneath him snarled and threw him aside, its black hat flying into the shadows. The imposter fought to a crouch, snarling and whining at the net of magic that held him to the ground.

Dru barked a harsh word in the *Verba Patiendi,* and the web disappeared from Leery. "Thanks," he muttered. "That was a real drag."

"Funny," Dru said without taking her gaze off the other wolf. "Pierre's better than we thought. I couldn't tell you apart. It even has the damn hat."

"Even I can't tell the difference," said Leery. "His scent is my scent. Everything..." He shook his head and got to his feet, wobbling a little from the weakness imparted by Dru's draining net. "How long until your spell makes him change?"

"With Pierre's spell in the mix, I don't know. Plus, whoever cast Pierre's spell has a lot of power. I can sense that much about the witch."

Leery walked toward the shadows and retrieved the imposter's hat. He came back to stand near Dru, the hat held modestly in front of him. "Come on, whoever you are. You're caught. There's no use chewing off your own leg."

The imposter treated them both to a weak snarl but fell back to the asphalt, head lolling. It growled and thrashed, slashing at the red strands of her energy-draining web.

"I don't want to hurt you," said Dru. "Stop struggling against the net."

One yellow eye rolled toward her, and the beast snarled, but it was a weak, pitiful sound rather than the fearsome ones from before.

"Listen," said Leery, kneeling down at the wolf's side. "We know you are being controlled by another. We've spoken with the man that crafted the spell."

The wolf rolled its head toward Leery, fixing him with its baleful gaze.

"You have to fight it." Leery waved at the illusion that covered its body. "Fight for your own identity. Fight for control of yourself."

The narrow, hateful squint left the imposter's eyes, and its head relaxed against the pavement.

"That's it," said Leery. "Let go of the anger; let go of that artificial hatred. Be yourself. No one can have power over who you are unless you let them have it. Take that power back."

Dru's net settled tighter and tighter against the imposter's flesh. The wolf sighed and closed its eyes, relaxing all of its muscles at once.

The *doppelgänger*'s image jittered to a stop, like a clockwork doll running down. It lay frozen for a heartbeat, then began to shimmer and shift as though something was tearing it to bits from within. When it came, the transformation crept across the imposter's form from the bottoms of its feet, washing upward like the ripple of a stone tossed into an otherwise still lake. Above the swell of transitioning flesh, Leery's frozen form still reigned, but beneath that line, matted midnight-blue fur and festering sores appeared.

"There you go, champ," said Leery. "Keep it going." He glanced back at Dru. "Anything you can do? Isolate him magically or something?"

Dru frowned down at the imposter, then shook her head. "No. He must sever the power that binds him from within. Nothing I can do."

As the rippling flesh neared the *doppelgänger*'s chest, the ripple slowed, seeming to shudder.

Leery crouched forward and dropped the hat to grab the imposter by the shoulders. "Fight it! You can do this. The power is yours, not theirs! Take it back!"

Smoke began to rise from the matted blue-black fur, and pustules broke across the imposter's abdomen, releasing the stench of death, of sour rot, of unchecked putrefaction. The smell of burning hair assaulted Leery's sensitive nose, mixing with the putrid scents from the bursting pus blisters, creating a noisome brume that invaded his sinuses, stung his eyes, and turned his stomach.

"Get back, Leery!" urged Dru. "I don't know what's happening, but it isn't good."

"We've got to help him!"

The rippling transformation lurched upward, revealing the trapped creature's chest...and furred breasts. The shedding of illusion progressed in fits and starts toward the dark blue creature's head.

"Er...*her*," said Leery, pulling back to squat on his haunches. "Didn't she seem like—"

"Pierre's spell."

"But..." Leery waved his hand at the creature lying before him. "What is she?"

Dru stepped closer and peered down, then shook her head and shrugged. "I've never seen anything like her."

"Pierre's spell..."

Dru sank next to Leery, watching her struggle against the spell. "Yes?"

"It's more than an illusion of me, isn't it?"

The imposter arched her back as though someone was strangling her as the transformation crossed her neck. Her heels pounded the macadam, and her fingers dug furrows across its surface. The blue-furred creature lifted her hands and pushed against her jaw as if Leery's appearance were a mask she could remove by force, but the fur of her shins and forearms burst into electric-blue flame, giving off an oily black smoke. She began to shriek and thrash, trying to roll but held fast by Dru's net.

"Good God," muttered Leery. He leaned forward and tried to beat out the flames that raced along her forearm, while Dru did the same to her shins.

The blue flames grew and grew, racing across the creature's true form, sizzling where wet pus dripped, crackling, and leaping where it encountered matted fur. The imposter released a series of rapid-fire chirps and squeals as the flames raced toward her head. She went up in mere seconds and was covered in bright blue flames before they could see her face.

"It's no use!" Dru yelled, pulling Leery away. "Some kind of failsafe—laid under Pierre's spell, I think."

"To keep her from being identified? For God's sake, why?"

The chirps and pitiful cries ceased, and the imposter lay still.

"Maybe there's a link between her identity and the caster."

"The sores…"

"Yes," said Dru. "Maybe we weren't supposed to know she was reanimated."

"But…" Leery shook his head. "Why make a purely supernatural creature like this into a zombie? I mean, she'd already have a set of powers, already have the ability to walk among us."

Dru's shoulders rose and fell. "Easier to control. In death, would she keep her natural powers?"

"I don't know the answer to that. I don't even know what she is."

"Neither do I. All I know is that was a terrible way to die."

"Better call Hendrix," said Leery. "Let her get at the remains as soon as possible. Maybe she can figure this mess out."

23

Hendrix stepped out of the black Town Car in a red sequined dress. She had a conical red-sequined hat tucked under her arm, and the hat bore various occult symbols worked in black sequins.

"Wow," said Leery, with a rakish smile. He wore his suit from earlier but hadn't bothered tying the tie.

"We don't all give our *entire* lives to the job, Leery," she said, her eyes zipping from his face to the taped-off crime scene and the sheeted figure behind him.

"Coven party?" asked Dru.

"Something like that," said Hendrix. "What's all this about?"

"Someone impersonating me. We don't know what she is." Leery stepped to the yellow crime scene tape and held it up so Hendrix could walk under it.

"*She*?"

Leery nodded. "The spell Dru's godfather crafted is a good one. She even *smelled* like me."

"So does a garbage scow." Hendrix stepped under the yellow tape and squatted on her heels next to the sheeted figure.

"Nice," said Leery, grinning.

"You'd better mean my joke."

"Oh, I do, doc. I do."

Liz glanced at him and then rolled her eyes. "Lech."

"Hey, anything for you, Hendrix. Just say the word."

Dru cleared her throat and walked over to Hendrix. "She was undead, we think, and covered in dark blue fur."

Hendrix flipped back the sheet and stared down at the corpse for a few seconds. "I'd say she's a ciguapa."

"Oh. That helps a lot," said Leery.

"Ciguapa are mountain creatures that torture climbers in the high mountains. They function like sirens, leading climbers astray, consuming their essence as they do so."

"I don't see any mountains around here, Hendrix."

"No, but that explains the sores, the reanimation."

"Of course, it does," said Leery with a sigh.

"Ciguapa are spiritually connected to the mountains they live on. Sort of like the Landvættir—land wights—of Scandinavia, but ciguapa are not spectral in nature. Take them off their plot of land, and they die horrible deaths."

"Then someone must have reanimated her?"

"Yes. There's no doubt of that."

"How sure are you that she's one of these mountain dwellers?" asked Dru.

"Ciguapa. Look here." Hendrix pointed at the soles of the creature's feet, which had strange pads on the heels and a large pad hanging from the great toe that would obscure the prints of the other toes. "The mundane myth is that ciguapa have their feet on backward, but anatomically, that's impossible, of course. These growths give their tracks the appearance of going in the opposite direction of travel, making them very hard to track without magic."

"Ah," said Dru. "I only wish we'd had more time to trace the spellcaster. To figure out who's behind all this."

"It's pretty clear who is behind this, Dru. The zees."

"Maybe," said Dru, tapping her fingernail against her teeth. "But why would Mama Rose Marie go to the trouble and expense of making this ciguapa into a zombie? The expense of tracking one down seems ridiculous, and she already has zombies at her disposal. Why not use one of them and make the anti-discovery spell stronger? Faster-acting?"

"Hey, who knows why a woman does anything, let alone a zombie crime boss." Leery looked down at the smoldering corpse.

"Certainly not crotchety old wolves," said Liz, tossing a wink at Dru. "Listen, I'll know more about this ciguapa after I do my work. I can probably figure out where she's from, and maybe where she's been."

"Any hope of tracing either Pierre's spell or the failsafe?"

Liz cocked her head to the side. "Anything's possible, Leery. What's *probable* is another question entirely."

"Right, right. What about the reanimation?"

Liz shrugged. "Maybe. It depends on the method. At the very least, I can compare it to the residue on Kay Soper to see if the person casting the reanimation was the same for both. Did you find her, by the way?"

"I did, but she got away when I came back to help Dru fight this thing," said Leery. "And I think you'll not only find the same master for both but that this ciguapa has traces of Mamaroneck all over her."

Liz lifted an eyebrow.

"He spent last night watching Rose Marie Van Dee's house."

"But she's in—"

"Yeah, but the zee running her family out of her house isn't."

"Ah," said Liz, returning her gaze to the ciguapa. "Well, give me six or eight hours."

"How about putting a rush on it?" asked Leery. "I'll owe you one."

Liz rose to her feet and turned to face him. "As long as you don't try to use it as an excuse to ask me out."

"Who? Me? Never."

"Right. Send her over to my office. I'm going home to change." Liz walked back to her car service and climbed in the back.

As the car drove away, Dru motioned for the Magical Examiner's van to clear away the body. "Well, Leery? What do we do now?"

"Feel like standing in the dark woods with me?"

Dru grinned. "You bring the coffee?"

"I'm offended you'd think otherwise."

24

Leery parked the cruiser half a mile down Forest Avenue, then led Dru on foot back toward Van Dee's McMansion. "Hey, is there any spell you can work that will let us hear the conversation on a cell phone?"

"Sure," said Dru. "Can I cast on the phone?"

"If you can do it by sight. The zee holding it tends to pace."

"That could be tough. Do you need to hear both sides of the conversation? It'd be much easier to put a spell on a window."

"That will do if you can't get the phone, but if we can hear the caller's voice, maybe that will give us a clue as to who is really calling the shots."

"I'll try," said Dru with a shrug.

"All I can ask." Leery pointed to a big copse of trees. "Back through there."

"Hold up a second," said Dru. She wrote sky-blue runes in the air and connected them with a golden pentagram. She uttered a word that sounded spidery and harsh in Leery's ears, then flicked the rune set-up in the air.

Watching the sky-blue dome settle over them, Leery asked, "Shield?"

"Camouflage. If anyone looks this way, they'll see dark shapes, but nothing more. If we don't move around too much, even someone staring right at us won't see anything alarming."

"That will make the night go easier."

"I aim to please."

Leery led her through the woods he'd surveilled the house from on the previous night, but given the illusion she'd cast, they got much closer to the massive home. Cars, trucks, and vans were parked helter-skelter in the drive and on the lawn, and zombies filled the visible parts of the house, milling around like at a party.

"Oh, that makes things more difficult. Do you see the woman with the phone?"

Leery squinted at the mass of zees, then pointed. "There she is. The tallish one with the phone glued to her ear."

"Let me see if I can catch her phone," said Dru. She stepped in front of Leery and sketched a rune set in the air. It glowed like they all did, but this time, it was a muted gray and had only three runes. She connected the symbols with a triangle and muttered another word in the *Verba Patiendi*, then stood with her hand poised as if to throw a shuriken or a tiny Frisbee side-arm. The rune set pulsed on a regular rhythm, spinning slowly a foot above her hand. "They are too close... Ah!" Dru snapped her wrist, and the pulsing gray figure flew away, following a slight arc. It shimmered through the big bay window, then zipped straight at the woman holding the phone.

At the last second, a tall male zombie stepped in the way, and the spell slid into his skull. He slapped his hand on the back of his head absently, as though swatting a pesky bug.

"Shit," Dru muttered.

"Hey, don't worry about it. That's a tough shot."

"I'll get it," Dru said in an iron tone. She repeated the process of casting the spell, then stood stock-still, leaning forward a little, her eyes glued to the woman with the phone. "It's timing, that's all."

Leery said nothing. His gaze traversed the taut lines of her muscles, her softer curves, her long, silky hair, the curved black horns.

"This would be easier without you ogling me."

"Oh, uh…" Leery cleared his throat and turned his gaze away. "Sorry."

"You can look as much as you want. Only later, okay?"

"Uh, right."

Dru flung her hand forward, coming up on her front foot and snapping her wrist. The gray pulsing spell leaped away, zipping along an arched trajectory, while Dru froze in place, her brow knotted with concentration. She leaned and twitched, trying to put English on the throw after it was in flight and totally out of her control.

Leery watched her move, a small smile on his face.

The spell dipped lower as it passed through the glass window, then curved higher again to skim over the heads of the zees milling around. Dru bit her lip and stepped to the side, waving her hand. The spell slipped past the last of the zees and slid into the phone.

"Yes!" Dru hissed. She whirled and threw her arms around Leery's neck, pressing close. "Did you see that?" she breathed in his ear.

"Uh, I... Uh, yes. What a shot," he croaked. Her hair smelled of summer heat and fresh flowers, and the rest of her smelled like sex. He squeezed his eyes shut and tried to think about something other than what his body wanted to think about.

Dru turned her face and lay her cheek on his chest. "This is nice."

"Well... Yeah, it's sort of like a dream, but..."

"I know," she said. She stood pressed against him for the space of a long sigh, then dropped her hands and stepped back, her eyes cast downward. "Let's...uh...listen to that call."

"Right," Leery said and cleared his throat. He turned his head away from her and drew a deep breath in through his nose, trying to clear away her marvelous scent. "Right."

Dru wrote in the air again, a pair of rune sets with three runes each, linked by a triangle. She activated the first and flicked it at Leery, then activated the second and put it on herself.

"And the woman?" asked a gruff female voice. "The volunteer?"

"She called from the City. The wolf almost had her, but the ciguapa pulled him away by attacking the partner." The woman inside the house had turned toward them, and her mouth moved with each word.

Dru turned to Leery, eyes widening.

Leery pursed his lips and shook his head.

"I take it she is making her way to you? We spent considerable power making her. It's time we see a return on our investment."

"She is, but she was nude and penniless when she revived—she awoke in some penthouse, though, and was able to steal some clothes and pocket change, but not enough for a car. She's taking the subway, so I expect—"

"Did your brain not revive with you?"

"Um, what?"

"I asked if you are brain dead, idiot." The woman's voice on the other end of the call turned ugly. "Send a fucking zee in a fucking car to get the fucking new girl, you fucking idiot."

"Oh. Yes, good idea."

"You think?" The sound of molars grinding together crackled across the line. "Don't make me replace you, Glenda."

"Sorry, Aida, I—"

"Aida? *Aida*? Keep on the way you're acting, and you'd better switch to Mama Rocha or just plain 'boss.'" Rocha's voice cracked like a whip, and Glenda shuddered as if struck by actual leather strands.

"Sorry, Mama Rocha."

"I'm not feeling confident here, Glenda. Do I need to send someone to...*help* you? Shondra, maybe?"

Inside the house, Glenda froze in mid-step, and her hand flew to her mouth. "No, Mama Rocha. I've got it under control. It was a momentary lapse."

"Uh-huh." Rocha's voice dripped with scorn. "Keep it in mind, yeah? Shondra Becker's always ready. I can have her out there in eight hours. Karma's a tiger when she gets riled, and I'd make sure she was riled before I sent her to you. You know she doesn't like you already."

"Yes, Mama Rocha." Glenda stood amidst the thronging zees in Van Dee's house, the only completely-still zombie in sight. "I'll get it together. There's just so much going on, and all these zees are—"

"Yeah? Well, that's the job, ain't it?"

"Yes, of course."

"We won't have this talk a second time."

"No, Boss. There won't be any need." Glenda stood up straight and dropped her hand away from her face.

"Now, what about the ciguapa?"

The woman inside Van Dee's house cringed. "She tried to shuck the spell. The palladium Karma cast fired. She's—"

"*She's gone*?" screamed Aida. "*My ciguapa is gone, and you stand there simpering? Are you fucking kidding me?*"

"Sorry, Boss Rocha. It's... You asked about the woman, and we got sidetracked, and—"

"*We* didn't get sidetracked, you silly little slit. You *neglected* to mention that my prized ciguapa pulled that fucker of a detective away and *got caught* and *tried to pull off the doppelgäng.* You. *NOT WE!*"

Glenda's eyes had closed during the diatribe, and her shoulders slumped.

"Hold on," said Rocha. The phone rustled as though she'd put her hand over the receiver, but what she said next was still clear enough. "Karma! Get out to the east coast. Yes, Mamaroneck. That bitch Glenda has fucked everything up. She's lost my ciguapa. What? Yeah, sure. Whatever you want." Then the phone rustled again. "Idiot?"

Glenda didn't answer.

"Glenda? Hello? Fucking idiot, you better not have hung up on me."

"I didn't," murmured Glenda.

"Right. Karma's on her way. When she gets there, you give her the phone, then you stand behind her and do whatever she wants you to do, even if it's dismembering yourself. You hear me, fucktard?"

"Yes, Mama Rocha. I'm... I'm sorry."

"Sorry? *Fuck you!*"

There was a screech that faded into silence, and Glenda dropped her hand to her side. She stood there, still as a statue, eyes squeezed shut.

Dru turned to Leery, one eyebrow arched.

"She's pleasant."

"Leery, why is the head of the Los Angeles Zombie mafia after you?"

"Maybe she likes Old Spice."

"No one *likes* Old Spice, Oriscoe."

"Then I guess I'm just lucky."

25

Dru and Leery entered the squad room at seven sharp, and Epatha Van Helsing stood in her office door, beckoning them. Leery couldn't keep the small, sheepish grin off his face as he crossed the room.

"Welcome back," Van Helsing said, her lips twitching with a suppressed smile.

"Thanks, Lieu. And thanks for that care package. It really hit the spot."

"Right."

Leery stopped within whispering distance. "Really sorry about the other day, Epatha," he said *sotto voce*.

"Why? What happened the other day?" She let the smile bloom on her face like a flower in spring.

"Hey, Lieu," said Dru.

"Nogan." Van Helsing nodded. "Inside, both of you." She disappeared and reappeared seated behind her desk. She gestured at her two visitor's chairs. "Tell me what you've discovered."

"We found the *doppelgänger*," said Dru. "Under the spell, it was one of the weirdest creatures I've ever seen. Dark blue fur, feet that—"

"Hendrix says it was a ciguapa," said Leery.

"Oh?" Van Helsing's ghostly eyebrows arched. "Expensive toy."

"Yeah, Liz said it was pretty rare."

"Then we're looking for a collector of exotic—"

"We know who owned it," said Leery with a grimace. "Your friend and mine, Aida Rocha."

"No!" breathed Epatha. "I thought her...uh...job took her out west?"

"Yeah. Los Angeles." Leery sighed and shrugged. "Looks like putting Mama Rose Marie away has created a vacuum in the locus. Mama Rocha seems interested in real estate over in Mamaroneck."

"That horrible wart?"

"Yeah. One thing it's got going for it, though... Floor to ceiling glass."

"And those dark trees all around. A stealthy wolf might see a lot," said Epatha with a grin.

"And if he's got a friend who can cast the right spells..."

"They might *hear* a lot," finished Dru.

"So that's how you know it's Mama Rocha."

"And they say you're getting slow," said Leery with a smile.

Van Helsing's eyes narrowed. "Who? Who says that?"

"Liz has the ciguapa and is running her tests," said Leery.

"Who, Leery?"

"Liz Hendrix."

"*You know what I mean*," hissed Van Helsing, flickering in and out of phase.

"Gotcha, Lieu." Leery leaned back in the chair and grinned.

"Is it too late to accept your resignation?"

Leery patted the pocket holding his credentials. "Far, far too late."

"Daddy always said my good nature would ruin me," said Epatha with a smile. "So. What do you need from me?"

"Rocha is in LA, but she's sending someone to—"

"Shondra Becker," Dru read from her notepad.

"—straighten Rocha's little trollop out. Karma Becker." He nodded at Dru.

"Karma is a nasty one. You be careful," she said to Dru. "She's mad as hops and willing to shake a flannin at a moment's notice."

"Uh…"

"She means she's 'excitable' and willing to fight it out at a moment's notice."

"That's what I said!" snapped Van Helsing. "Not my fault you two don't speak properly."

"Right, Lieu. Listen, we're going to need help in LA."

Van Helsing nodded. "I can put in a call, but McCoy'll have more capital out there. He can go through the LA Locus Magister's office, or maybe through the Covenancy Magister's office, if he hasn't burned all his bridges there." She nodded and glared at her phone for a moment before stabbing at the speakerphone button with a translucent finger. She got it on the third try and dialed Sam's office line.

"What is it, Epatha?" Sam McCoy asked by way of greeting.

"Sam, Leery, and Dru have a cross-locus issue. We could use your help."

McCoy picked up the phone on his end. "I've got an opening statement to prepare. What do they need?"

"Hello, McCoy," said Leery. "We've got Aida Rocha throwing her weight around in the Van Dee Family."

"What's left of it, you mean."

"Right. She's got a pigeon in Mamaroneck operating out of Van Dee's mansion, and she's sending an enforcer to line up all the ducks."

"Enforcer?"

"Shondra Becker."

"Oh, she's a piece of work."

"That's what I told them."

"I'm guessing you want cross-jurisdiction cooperation?"

"I'd rather have them at my beck and call, but—"

"It's LA, Detective. You'll be lucky if they return your calls on the same day you make them. I'll see what I can do."

"Thanks, Sam."

"I'm preparing for the Mad Dog Telep case, so I'll have Angie follow up once we get it all set up."

"She's easier on the eyes anyway," said Leery.

"I'll tell her you said so, you old wolf."

"You do that, McCoy."

"Is Karma still gunning for you?"

"Probably," said Leery. "But, hey, what's a little ass-kicking between arch-enemies?"

26

They spent the rest of the morning putting out APBs for Kay Soper and Shondra Becker, a.k.a. Karma, and setting up the task force with the LA Locus Sheriff's Department in order to keep the LA chapter of *Noster Est* surveilled. It wasn't glamourous work, but at least it kept Leery close to the coffee maker. His phone rang as he was coming back with a fresh cup—his thirteenth of the morning—and he dashed to get it.

He slid into his chair, holding his coffee cup out to the side and staring at it with intense concentration. He grabbed the receiver with his other hand and pressed it to his ear. "What?"

"When the hell were you going to clue me in, Oriscoe?"

"What? Who... Evie?"

"You know damn well who it is, Oriscoe!" said Yvonne. "Tell me, did you even think about giving me a call? An email? Don't you think you should let the OC bureau know that the Zombie mafia from LA is moving into our locus? Don't you think—"

"Wait a minute, Evie. Just wait a minute."

Yvonne snapped her mouth shut, but Leery could hear her rapid breathing.

"Listen, we've been a little busy over here. We're interfacing with the LM's office, both here and in LA, and we're setting up—"

"Yeah. Right. No need to involve the Occult Cabal unit in your little task force."

"—a working..." Leery cleared his throat. "Oh. Yeah."

"And Aida Rocha? You didn't think we'd be interested in hearing that she's got zees in our jurisdiction?"

"Right. I get it, Evie. You can quit busting my balls now. I apologize profusely."

"Yeah, well..."

"Evie, there's something else. Mama Rocha sent Shondra Becker to—"

"Oh, for fuck's sake, Leery! *Karma*?"

"Yes. Karma is on her way to Mamaroneck." The line hissed and scratched in Leery's ear. "Evie? You still there?"

"Yes, Oriscoe, I'm still here. I'm just trying to figure out how I can murder you and not get caught."

"Can't be done. Too many people love me, Evie."

"Yeah, right."

"Come on over here, Evie. We've already talked about setting up a joint unit task force with you guys, and the lieu is onboard."

Again, the scratching, hissing static-filled Leery's ear for a moment. "Right. I'm on my way. Tell Van Helsing to go ahead and make it official."

"Already done." Yvonne hung up, and Leery dropped the phone in its cradle and glanced at Dru.

"Trouble?"

"Nah. I've just got go in there and convince Van Helsing to set up a joint task force with OC, that's all."

Dru laughed. "Good luck."

"Not coming with me?"

"No way in Hell."

"Chicken?"

"No, smart."

27

By the time Evie arrived from 1 PP, Leery was back, and Van Helsing had stopped appearing next to his desk to yell at him for a few seconds. Dru had even stopped grinning when he wasn't looking.

Evie got off the elevator and walked into the squad room, her eyes on Leery's face. "Oriscoe," she said.

"Hello, Evie," said Dru.

"Nogan." She darted a glance at Dru, then cut her eyes back to Leery. "Is it all set? Everything's official?"

"Sure. Van Helsing called your lieutenant and 'borrowed' you. We've just been waiting for you to get here so we can pop over to the ME's office for an update on our *doppelgänger*."

"Then let's go," said Evie.

Leery and Dru got their coats, and the three headed toward the elevator, but as the doors opened, Van Helsing appeared. "You've got another body," she said.

"What? But the *doppelgänger* is—"

"Guess the imposter killed this one last night before you got her, Oriscoe. Your victim is in The Ramble Cave. Get over there and see what you can see."

"Right. Are we sure the crimes are related?"

Van Helsing shrugged. "Hinton got a description from the victim. You can guess who it sounds like."

Leery grimaced and shook his head.

28

Jenn Hinton stood outside the sealed entrance to the cave, waiting on them, tapping her foot, and looking at her watch. "About time," she muttered.

"What's the matter, nemesis? Got a hot date with a shoe salesman?"

"Funny, Bandit."

Dru walked to the head of the steps leading down to the cave's closed-off entrance and looked around. "Where's the body? Van Helsing said it was at the cave."

Jenn shook her head. "No, I bet she said it was *in* the cave." She shrugged and stepped past her to descend the stone staircase. At the bottom of the stairs, she turned and glanced up at them. "Coming?"

"But the cave is sealed off. Has been forever. Everyone knows that."

"To mundanes..." Hinton turned toward the narrow passage between the thick rock slabs and, turning her massive feet sideways, she crab-walked to the wall of stone bricks. She tapped three stones in what appeared to be a random pattern. Each stone lit from within, and a low-frequency rumble sounded from beneath their feet.

Dru glanced up at Leery. "Did you know about this?"

Leery shook his head. "I'm just a coffee-swilling werewolf. No one tells me about the cool places to go."

The stone wall blocking the cave's entrance began to unfold, stones turning in place, then flipping back into the darkness beyond. Once the grinding rumble finished, the entrance was free of mortar and stone bricks. Jenn crab-walked into the shadowed interior without a word, and the others followed.

Jenn led them down a short corridor into a round room, that, in everyday situations, would have been cool and dark, but was lit up by massive glowing spheres of magical light. In the center of the circular chamber lay a woman's body. Her throat had been torn out the way Kay Soper's had, and her torso bore the same kinds of mutilation, but she had defensive wounds on her forearms—bites and long, ragged tears in her skin.

"Well, the terminal wounds look the same, at least."

Hinton nodded. "She described you perfectly, Oriscoe."

"Oh, this one kept it together enough to gossip, eh? No hysterics? No 'oh I can't possibly tell you anything because I'm in on it?'"

Hinton grimaced. "Well, the first one's trauma seemed genuine. Sue me."

"Hey, we've all been there, nemesis." Leery turned and examined the walls and floor. "Dump job, huh?"

"Yes, she was killed outside, then carried in here."

"Why?" asked Dru. "If the point is to frame Leery, then why hide the body?"

"And what's this place used for? It's closed off unless you know the right spell, I guess, but to what end?"

"It's used for certain rituals."

"Oh?" asked Leery. "That's so interesting. And informative! Kind of like saying 'we use this for things.' Anything *helpful* to add, Hinton?"

She turned a flat gaze on him. "Sure. Right after you start telling the dark secrets of the Pack."

"Come on, Hinton, don't give me that crap. Dru didn't even know this place was here, and if *anyone* would know the dark secrets of the Gehenna set, it would be her."

"Demon is my race, Bolt. It doesn't define the full extent of my life."

"Cute, Bigfoot. So, what? It's used by the secret society of CSI technicians?"

Hinton scoffed. "Sure."

Leery shook his head. "Is it a medium thing?"

"No, it's pretty large for a cave."

"Funny, Hinton. Hear me laughing?"

"Think about it, Oriscoe. I'm sure you'll get it in twenty years or so."

"Whatever. Since you can't answer my question, try Dru's. Why would someone hide a body here if the intent is to frame me for the murder?"

"That's for you detectives to answer," said Jenn in a schoolmarm's tone. "I'm just here to commune with the dead."

"Speaking of which, let's get on with it."

"Right." Jenn bowed her head for a moment, and then she summoned the victim's spirit. "Detectives Oriscoe, Nogan, and Evans, meet Linda Rodgers. Ms. Rodgers, the detectives."

"'Meetcha," said Rodgers. "You gonna find this asshole, or do I have to haunt your station?"

"We already did," said Leery. "We ran into her last night, right after dark. She didn't survive."

"Right after dark? Nuh-uh. No way," said Linda. "Wrong guy."

"It wasn't a guy at all," said Dru. "Though the spell obscured that. It was a zombie—"

"Well, the guy that killed me was definitely a guy. A werewolf guy, sure, but I know the difference between males and females regardless of species, thank you very much."

"No," said Leery. "There was powerful magic in place that may have—"

"Listen, sparky, and listen good. I lived three hundred and forty-seven years on this planet and practiced magic for three hundred and thirty-three of those years. When I say this was a guy, I mean it was a guy. A male."

"The spell—"

"Are you deaf, sparky? I told you. I'm a witch, and I saw through the little obscuration spell. Underneath it, he was a werewolf, but he started this life like you or me—a human. A part of his spell tried to bind me to my body, but I will not be used in that way, and I dispelled both before I lost my breath."

Leery glanced at Dru and shrugged.

"The...*doppelgänger* we...uh...dealt with last night was a ciguapa."

"A zombie ciguapa!" The spirit barked harsh laughter. "Well, there you go. Different killer. A werewolf killed me, and here's a clue you've missed so far: he was *alive*. He was being controlled until I died, then he howled and ran off toward the lake. That brought out the person driving him—one of them Orthodox Jews, like them that lives over in Borough Park. You know the type. Hat, funny side-whiskers, dressed in all black."

"Yeah, I know the type," said Leery. "And you're sure this wasn't just another illusion?"

"That's what I said, ain't it? He had a lame obfuscation spell like the first one, but I'd already seen past it with his friend, so it didn't work."

Leery sighed and threw up his hands. "Fine." He turned to Dru and shrugged. "Maybe the zees recruited a new guy from outside the locus."

Dru turned a bright gaze on Rodgers. "Was this Black Hat undead?"

Rodgers shook her head. "He was alive, too. He smelled a lot like this one over here." She jerked her chin at Oriscoe.

"Hey, Old Spice is a popular scent—"

"Not that, sparky. The *wolf* part."

Leery snapped his lips shut and dropped his gaze to the floor.

"You were attacked by a wolf under the mental control of a Hassid, who was also a werewolf, both of whom pretended to look like *another* werewolf?"

"Yep, that's it. The first attacked me looking like one wolf, but after I dispelled it and ran off, I died. The second one came out, not knowing I could see through his disguise, and when he saw I was dead, he dropped the illusion. He was another wolf, and then he changed into the Jew and got himself dressed."

Leery squeezed his eyes shut.

"Leery?" asked Dru.

He shook his head.

"What is it?" asked Evie. "What's the matter, Oriscoe?"

Leery heaved a sigh. "There's only one other Pack Brother who's a Hassid," he murmured.

"Oh, shit," said Dru.

"That's right," said Leery.

"When was the last time you... Maybe it's like you said. Maybe he's from another locus, recruited by the zees."

Leery waved his hand in the air. "Well, thanks, Rodgers. We'll hunt down your killer, no need to haunt us."

"You'd better," she said. "I'm not above spending a century rattling around in your precinct house."

"No, no," said Leery. "I think I know the man controlling the wolf who attacked you."

"Oh. Good."

"The only real question is why."

"Seems like your friend wanted to send you a message," said Linda. "Good thing he picked someone who could tell you all this."

"Yeah..." mumbled Leery. "Why would he do that? He'd know I'd get this case..."

"Leery," said Dru. "The spells were crafted by Pierre using *Kabbalic* magic."

"Yeah, I know that, Dru."

"And why use magic like that? Mama Rocha has a ton of black magicians at her disposal, right? Why go so far to find an archaic form of magic?"

"Well, for one thing, Hendrix couldn't recognize it."

"Sure, but she would have, in time. And this thing is targeted at *you*, right? You thought you recognized the magic right away. 'Smells like Kabbalah,' you said."

"As fascinating as this is," said Rodgers. "I've got dead-girl stuff to do. You need me for anything else?"

Hinton arched an eyebrow at Oriscoe, and he shook his head. "You may go. Thank you for coming."

"Sure." Linda turned a blazing gaze on Oriscoe. "Don't let this guy off just because you know him. I can haunt you as easily as I can haunt a police station."

"Go on," said Leery. "Let us get to work."

Linda Rodgers nodded once and disappeared.

"Come on," said Leery, turning toward the entrance. "Let's go talk to Hendrix. I know where he'll be later this afternoon, we can catch him then. We've got an hour or so to kill. See you later, Sasquatch."

29

Leery drove in silence, ignoring two different Starbucks shops, not even sipping the coffee that sat in the cupholder. He sighed two or three times on the trip, but no one spoke. He pulled into the garage beneath the Health Department building and found a space reserved for official vehicles. He parked and got out.

"Come on," he said. "Let's go see what Hendrix has for us."

"Right," said Evie.

"Leery..."

"Not now, Dru." He turned and went to call the elevator.

"Something's wrong," said Dru.

"Let him process it. He gets quiet like this when things hit too close to home."

"Am I right in assuming the one Pack Brother who's a Hassid is the one that bit him?"

Evie nodded. "The one and only 'bus driver' as Leery likes to call him."

"Cripes. This case... I picked the wrong week to quit sniffing glue."

Evie turned to her, eyebrows arched with surprise, a small smile on her lips. "I'm impressed someone so young knows that reference."

"Hey, I like comedy as much as the next girl. And *Airplane!* was voted the funniest comedy ever in 2012."

"Still."

Dru rolled her eyes. "Okay, okay. I'm not as young as I may look. Satisfied?"

Evie tipped her a wink. "Can one become a succubus? Like, I don't know, convert, or something?"

"Sorry. You have to be born to it. Vampire, on the other hand..."

The elevator dinged, and after Evie got done with her shudder, they hurried to join Leery inside the car. He pressed the button, staring straight ahead, his usual smile absent, and they rode in silence to Liz's floor.

Pushing through the double doors leading from her workroom, Hendrix beckoned them. "It's about time. You called forty minutes ago, Dru."

"We had a stop to make," said Leery. "Another victim."

Liz stared up at him for a moment, then nodded. "Bad?"

"What do you have, Hendrix?" asked Leery.

"Right. The ciguapa has been dead for a long time, but she was preserved, cared for. Someone loved the idea of having such a rare creature and spared no expense."

"Why risk her in a caper like this?" asked Evie.

Liz shook her head. "Can't answer that one."

"The Zombie mafia has sent an enforcer," said Leery. "Shondra Becker? Goes by Karma?"

Liz shook her head. "Never heard of her."

"You've probably examined some of her victims. She used to be a big-time New Orleans hoodoo queen before she went exclusive with *Noster Est*. Now, she's a hitter and an enforcer," said Evie. "Nasty piece of work."

"Is she a zombie then?"

"No, but there's a rumor she's discovered an immortality ritual that actually works, and she made her bones—if you'll pardon the bad pun—raising skeletons to kill her rivals."

"Necromancer, then."

"Yes, and her arts attracted some heavies from *Noster Est* about fifteen years ago. She's not a zombie, so she holds no rank in the organization, but most zees are deathly afraid of her—and with good reason, she can deanimate as easily as reanimate."

Liz nodded and led them back inside her workroom. She had her prismatic window set up, and she pointed at it. "This ciguapa was reanimated by a master of the art—likely this Karma woman—and maintained at regular intervals. In fact, though she's been dead for at least two years, she only became putrefactive a few weeks ago. You can see the conglomeration of magic residue here and here." She pointed at two spots, one between the ciguapa's breasts, and one under her left arm. Unlike the rainbow shimmer of the residue she'd found on the *doppelgänger*'s victim, the residue was a greasy black smudge on the midnight-blue fur.

"That's a lot of power expended," said Dru. "Expensive, if you can't do the work yourself."

"Aida Rocha's no necromancer," said Leery.

"But Karma seems to answer to her."

"Karma's willing to do work for anyone with the right number of zeros," said Evie. "It was

Rocha who made it known that Karma is off-limits to anyone else."

"And how did she react to that proclamation?" asked Dru.

"Intel says she went along, but there's no telling how she really feels about the restriction. Financial records show she's done pretty well out of the deal, though."

"How long has she been exclusive?"

"Seven years."

Leery grunted. "Traditional term for a contract of servitude."

"Yep," said Evie.

"Any chance Karma is the owner of the ciguapa?"

Liz shrugged. "Not my department."

"My best guess would be no. Sure, Becker has the power. She could do the work herself, but why? It would serve her better to give the thing away, to sell it." Evie shook her head. "The intel we have indicates Shondra Becker is into luxury items—fancy cars, plush houses, furs, like that. If this was a ciguapa fur coat, I'd believe it, but a live creature? Nah."

Leery chopped his hand through the air. "This is all speculation. What do you need to figure out if Karma was the necromancer that maintained the creature post-mortem?"

Liz tilted her head and looked at him for the space of three or four breaths. "Do you have someone else in mind?" she asked in a quiet voice.

Leery dropped his gaze. "Is it..." He shook his head. "Could this necromancy be Kabbalic-based like the identity-theft spell itself?"

Liz pursed her lips. "That's a tough question, given the length of time that has passed since the last incantation."

"Oh, that's just great, Hendrix. Hey, here's an idea. How about you give us something useful for a change? You know, something other than conjecture?"

"Leery, that's not—"

"That's not fair? Yeah? So what? Nothing in life is fair!" Leery whirled and stomped back toward the elevator. "I'll be in the car when you're done *playing fair.*"

Dru watched him stride off, her mouth hanging open a little.

Liz dropped her gaze to the floor. "Where'd that come from?"

"The last victim described the person who killed her, and—"

"But we know there's a *doppelgänger* spell in play. No one—"

"She was an old witch. She saw right through the spell, but it was too late. The perp was another werewolf this time. A Hassidic werewolf."

"But there are only two..." Liz's gaze darted toward the elevator. "Oh."

"What else can you tell us, Liz?" asked Evie.

Liz turned back to the ciguapa. "Mind control," she said. "Someone had this one wrapped up tight, and for a long time."

"You'd expect that from a captive creature of wild fae, wouldn't you?"

"I'd expect some degree of mind control, yes, but the degree to which control was exerted here..." She shook her head. "I'm amazed that she had enough will power at the end to try and break free."

"Mind control," murmured Dru. "Pierre said he was asked to weave mind control into one of the spells Rocha demanded of him, to control a Hassidic wolf." She shrugged. "At the time, I assumed it was to control Leery like the fetch's compulsion a while back." She shook her head and heaved a sigh. "Now..."

"Yes," said Liz. "Now we know who the spell was for. Leery's bus driver."

"And we know why only one of the spells needed mind control. The ciguapa was already under the effects of brainwashing."

Liz nodded. "It appears so."

"I assume you can no more tell us about the controller as you can the caster of the identity spell?"

"That's right," said Liz. "And for the same reasons." She glanced at the doors. "Listen, I'll put a rush on this second victim. I'll let you know if the magical residues match."

"Thanks, Liz," said Dru. "And sorry about Leery."

Liz tossed her head. "No problem. I'd be a mess in his place."

30

Leery was already in the car and drumming his fingers on the steering wheel when Dru and Evie came down in the elevator. Neither woman spoke as they climbed in the car and he turned the ignition. "I'll make it up to her," he said in a quiet voice.

"She understands, Oriscoe," said Evie.

"But an apology wouldn't hurt," said Dru.

"Right." Leery put the car in reverse and backed out of the spot.

"So… How do we find your maker, Leery?"

"That's no problem," he said. "I've got a list of places he'll be this afternoon."

"How do you know all that?"

Leery held up his phone and shook it back and forth. "It's all on the interwebs, Dru. My 'maker' as you call him, is the general of one of the Mitzvah Tanks in the afternoons."

"Mitzvah Tanks?"

"Yeah, you saw one the day we met. Outside Riverside Park."

"The day we…" Her eyes brightened. "You mean that horrible RV? The one with the rabbi's picture?"

"Right. Certain Hassidim use vehicles like that as 'education and outreach' centers and minagogues to reconnect with 'questioning' Jews."

"And your…friend drives one of these?"

"Friend. Ha." Leery shook his head, then tapped his phone. "It says here his tank will be on the south side of Washington Square Park until three."

"Washington Square Park? You think he'll be driving one of these tanks today? After he puppeted a murder last night?"

"He doesn't know anyone knows about that, remember? He thinks he got away with it."

"And your... Look, I'm tired of saying 'your maker' and having you sneer at me. So give. What the hell is your bus driver's name?"

Leery grimaced at the traffic ahead. "Rabbi Menachem Katzen."

Dru raised an eyebrow. "Your werewolf maker is a rabbi?"

"Yeah. Haven't you heard the joke?"

"The joke?"

"A rabbi walks into a bar with a wolf. He's a Hassid, with *tzitzits*, the hat, the *payot*, everything. The bartender looks at him and says, 'Hey, where'd you get that thing.' The wolf answers, 'Brooklyn, there are lots of them there.'" He didn't smile or laugh, only kept glaring out the window.

"Maybe that would be funny another time," murmured Dru.

Leery shrugged. "Listen, both of you. I know Menachem—better than I want to. He's been after me for years to get serious, to 're-engage with Judaism,' as he puts it. I don't know what's going on here, but he's not the type of man to go around orchestrating the death of anyone."

"And yet Linda Rodgers couldn't have been any clearer."

"Yeah," grunted Leery. "It doesn't make sense." He turned from 2nd Avenue onto West 4th Street and began picking through the one-way traffic moving in the opposite direction.

"Christ, Leery. Will you ever learn to drive? At least put on the spinners," said Evie.

"Hey, we're cops. If we can't drive the wrong way on a one-way street, who can?"

"Isn't that kind of the point of one-way streets? That no one is supposed to go the wrong way?"

Leery glanced at Dru and flashed a weak smile at her. "Amateur."

By some feat of magic, they made it to Washington Square Park without killing anyone. Leery pulled up on the curb and swung the Crown Vic into the bike path across from the Judson Memorial Church.

He killed the ignition and waved his hand toward the front of the car. "Look, Dru, they saved us a parking space."

"Uh, yeah." Dru looked at him askance. "I'm glad you're feeling better."

"Right. Let's go talk to Menachem. But let me do the talking. If he asks you if you are a Jew, say 'no.' Unless you *want* an hours-long lesson on the Torah. And above all else, don't mention your mother."

Dru shrugged as Leery stepped from the car. She watched him adjust his belt and turn toward the NYU School of Law, then followed his gaze toward the florescent green RV parked at the curb across the street. "MITZVAH TANK" was emblazoned on the side in bright red, with the "LIBRARY AND RESOURCE CENTER" underneath. Without waiting for them, Leery set off at a fast walk toward the tank, his long stride gobbling up the distance.

"Your mother?" asked Evie.

"Come on, Evie," said Dru as she, too, got out of the car and turned toward the Mitzvah Tank. "Let's go keep Leery out of trouble."

"Heh. That's pretty near to impossible, hon."

"I know, but a girl's got to try."

31

By the time Dru climbed the steps into the RV, Leery had a short man dressed in black pinned on the tweed couch, putting on cuffs. Several Jewish men stood around muttering and pointing at the spectacle.

"I told you, Mendel. Screw around, and I'm taking you in."

"Relax, Lerome! Relax! I only suggested we pray together!" Several long black leather straps that supported a small, leather-clad box lay on the floor at the foot of the couch. "I wanted to put a few *tefillin* on you! It's a mitzvah, and you know it! Well, a part of you knows it, at least."

"Maybe so, Menachem, but part of *you* knows why *I'm* here this afternoon, and you know it's not to pray!"

"What are you talking about?"

"You were seen last night. You know, when you brainwashed some poor wolf into committing murder."

"What? I have no idea—"

"Give it up, Rabbi. *She was a witch*! She dispelled your *doppelgäng* spell! She saw right through you."

Menachem rested his head on the arm of the chair. "That doesn't... Leery, it was only a nightmare!"

Oriscoe grimaced and pulled the rabbi to a sitting position. Katzen's gaze bounced from Leery's face to Evie's, finally coming to rest on Dru. "Are you Jewish?" he asked.

"In a way, maybe." Dru dropped her gaze away from the rabbi's eyes.

"Drop the mitzvah routine, Menachem. Are you seriously going to run with the 'it was all a dream' excuse?"

"Lie to you, I would? You know better, Lerome Oriscoe. That is an *aveyre,* even if you've lost your way."

"Yeah, and driving someone else to commit murder with Kabbalic magic is also a sin, Rabbi. Unfortunately for you, it's also against the law and comes with a long, all expenses paid trip to one of the Locus of New York's fine dungeons."

"Trip-shrip! Guilty of nothing, I am. A dream, it was!"

"Tell it to the dead witch in The Rambles, Rabbi."

An expression of confusion passed over Menachem's face. "No, no, no, no. Don't be such a *knacker* in front of your pretty little woman."

"First, she's not my 'pretty little woman,' she's my partner. Another cop, Rabbi, capiche? Second, I'm not the one pretending to be a big deal. I'm not driving around in an electric lime of an RV shouting at every *apikoyres* I see."

"Gentlemen," said Evie. "Let's everyone pull it back a notch. Wouldn't a nice conversation at the Twenty-seventh Precinct be better than this shouting in the street?"

"In the street, we are?" scoffed Menachem. "You want the precinct house? No, I say! I have work!"

"Not today, you don't," said Leery as he pulled Menachem to his feet and propelled him toward the sidewalk outside the door. "You don't have a choice anymore."

"Leery, Leery, listen to me! What you claim I did, does it sound like me? I'd as soon murder someone as chew off my own paws!"

"Stick to that story, Menachem. See where it goes." Leery helped the older man down the steps, one hand on his shoulder, the other on his elbow. "I did mention the eyewitness, didn't I?"

"Why are you doing this, Leery?"

"It's my job, Menachem. You broke the law, and now, you're caught."

32

Van Helsing appeared next to Leery as he poured foul precinct-house coffee into his dirty mug. "You're going to get a virus doing that."

"What, I should live forever?"

"Are you okay?"

"Why shouldn't I be okay?"

"Don't do that, Leery," said Epatha. "Don't keep me at arm's length."

Leery sighed without looking up from his coffee. "We both know the people you think are above it are the ones that break your heart."

"Yes, that's true."

"I can't figure it, Lieu. He's got no reason to be involved in this. He's never so much as rubbed elbows with *Noster Est.*"

"That you know of."

Leery loosed another sigh and swirled his coffee to disrupt the rainbow sheen that formed on its surface. "Even if they joined his flock, Lieu, he wouldn't stand for it."

"What's Dru say?"

Leery wagged his head to the side and back. "She reminded me that Pierre created a spell specifically for a Hassid 'of great faith' but with a vulnerability."

"And this rabbi? What's his vulnerability?"

Leery swigged his coffee. "Me."

"Leery, that's—"

"No, it's true, Lieu, and you and I both know it." Leery grimaced and took another jolt from his cup. "They should use this to clean battery terminals."

"I think the motor pool *does*. Would Katzen break his beliefs for anyone, Leery?"

"No, but he's in this because of me. Because of what I did to Aida's sidekick."

The lieutenant shook her head. "I checked, Leery. Sweet little Mary Anne made a full recovery. I mean, she's still a zombie, but the prison hospital ward got her new limbs and grafted some skin on her neck and belly."

Leery frowned at his coffee.

"She's *fine*, Oriscoe. Mama Rocha has no reason to hold a grudge. Mary Anne Davoli should have let you arrest her. She shouldn't have pulled that silver dagger, and she shouldn't have attacked Mesmerina."

"Yeah, but she did, and I'll bet you a box of ghost doughnuts that Mama Rocha *does* hold a grudge, no matter how good my reasons were. And you know those dungeon necromancers don't put forth much effort for the sake of a prisoner's good looks. I'll bet you another box of doughnuts that 'sweet little Mary Anne' looks like a walking train wreck."

Van Helsing treated him to a long, penetrating look. "That's as may be, Leery, but she's mobile. Her guts aren't hanging out. If Rocha is so shallow...well, that's on her."

"Anyway, we'd better get in there before Menachem converts Dru and Evie."

Epatha nodded and led him to the observation room in silence, floating in front of him like a mother duck leading a wayward duckling. Angie Carmichael was already in the room and had the intercom volume turned up.

"But, I did *no such thing!*"

"Mr. Katzen," said Dru with a sigh. "We've run the tests, tied the magic to you. That plus the eyewitness..." She sucked her teeth. "Your fate is as clear as a neon sign in the pitch black of a moonless midnight."

"*Bobkes*!"

Evie leaned across the table, staring at him with an earnest expression. "So, it was all a dream? Rabbi, tell us about your dream. Tell us everything you remember."

"Yes, let's waste time on more *bobkes*. Dreams are nothing but mental burps, Detective."

"Maybe so but humor me. You said you dreamed you were walking in The Rambles, and you saw a young wolf run off toward the lake..."

"Yes, yes. Fine. In my dream, I was walking through The Rambles, as you say. It makes no sense for me to be there. Before the park, the last I remember was taking a call as I prepared for bed. I had covered my eyes for the *Shema* when the annoyance rang at me. Irritated, I was, with whoever called. I—"

"You don't remember who called?"

"I should be so lucky. Then I could tell his name to you, and you could go hassle him for all of the afternoon."

"Go on," said Evie.

"I checked the phone this morning because I couldn't remember what the call was about. A waste of time, that call must have been. But there was no call in my call log, so maybe it too was part of my dream.

"So, there I was, walking in the park at night, just waiting to be mugged, God forbid! I saw this youngster, this *bonditt*, I know from the Pack. He was doing something, tearing at something with his teeth like a savage. I called to him. What, I don't recall. A greeting, perhaps. He looked at me, then ran off toward the lake.

"I continued to walk through the woods, like night is not the time for sleeping. I stumbled across a woman's body, and I think to myself, '*This* I need yet?'

"Then I understood that I was not only walking in the woods, but that I was...*ahem*...dressed in fur, and I regained my form and dressed in the clothes I found in a bag at my feet. You see? This is a nonsense dream."

"What happened after that?"

"Why, I walked home and went to bed. It was late, even in my dream."

"Let me interpret your dream, Rabbi Katzen," said Evie as she glanced at Dru, who stared at Katzen as though he'd grown a tail.

In the observation room, Leery murmured, "Here it comes. Watch this. It's one of Evie's best tricks."

"Get lost. Who needs it?" said Menachem.

"Come on, Rabbi. Humor me. It's just a game I like to play. A parlor trick." Evie's voice had taken on a soothing monotone, and she tapped the table in a steady rhythm with the nail of her index finger.

"Silliness."

"Here's what I think. You *remember* the phone call, so let's assume it really happened. Then—"

"But there's no record!"

"Those records aren't infallible. Let's say—for the sake of argument—that someone called you and cast a spell, a compulsion, on you over the phone. Let's say that part of it was to believe it was only a dream."

"Plain talk: you've lost your marbles."

"Sure, sure, but play along. So you think it's a dream, but the things you dreamed about really happened. Don't you recall what happened before you got to The Rambles?" Her voice never strayed from the soothing monotone.

"Like what?"

"Like maybe you went to this young wolf's house—or maybe just called him—and cast a spell of your own."

"You see, this is where you are wrong. The Kabbalah isn't magic as you perceive it. It's—"

"Sure, that's fine. Let's say someone else *gave* you the spell. Someone who is versed in spellcrafting." Her index finger went up and down, up and down.

Katzen threw up both hands. "You think I don't see what you're doing? Am I so stupid?"

"It's a thought exercise, Rabbi. To prompt your memory, to help you recall details of your dream. I'm just giving you context." Her gaze rested on his eyes, and her breath went in and out in time to her incessant tapping.

"You're giving me a headache, if you'll pardon the expression. It shouldn't happen to a dog!" But even as he said it, Katzen's respiration fell into time with hers.

"Play along, Menachem," said Dru in her sweet voice.

The rabbi glanced at her, and his expression softened. "Okay by me. For you, *anything, bubeleh.*"

"Oh, boy," said Leery. "She's turned on the voltage."

"Okay, so you've taken the call, heard the spell placed on you, contacted the young wolf, and cast the spell you'd been given. What happens between then and when you are walking in The Rambles?" Evie sat perfectly straight, as still as a statue, all except her index finger, tap, tap, tapping on the table's core.

Menachem's gaze caressed Dru, and she smiled at him. "Yes," he said. "After I repeat the spell I'm given, I'm to follow him, to make sure he completes his task. Someone else has done something...*wrong,* and the woman on the phone wants for a distraction to be made in the Park while she puts things right."

"And then?"

Katzen darted an annoyed glance at Evie, then his gaze twisted to the mirror. "Is that Lerome I smell? Him and his coffee. Feh!"

"Ignore him," said Dru in a singsong voice. "Focus, *bubeleh.*"

"Not too much, Dru," muttered Leery. "Go easy."

Menachem turned his gaze back toward Evie, and a distrustful look entered his eyes.

"After you've made the distraction, then what?" Evie leaned forward at the waist, bringing her face closer to Katzen's, her eyes boring into his.

A low, teeth-rattling growl erupted from the rabbi's grimacing mouth, and he pushed his upper body away from the table. "Nothing...but...a...dream," he panted.

"Come now, Rabbi," crooned Evie. "Every story needs a beginning, a middle, and an end. What happened next?"

Katzen's lips rippled and twitched, and he bared his teeth at her but said nothing.

"*Bubeleh*," murmured Dru in a voice that would have melted the heart of the most cold-hearted of serial killers. "Tell me."

Menachem glanced at her, eyes wild, and snapped at her like a vicious dog. His eyes rolled in their sockets, bouncing from the two detectives to the window, to the mirror, to the door. He shook his head as though trying to rid himself of a pesky fly.

"Rabbi, look at me," said Evie in a voice as relaxing as a calm day at the lake.

Katzen twisted his head back and forth, teeth gritted, the skin of his nose bunched up, but his gaze found hers and locked on it.

"It's simple, Rabbi. You've fulfilled the wish for a distraction that your midnight caller requested. You've done a good job and gotten away without leaving living witnesses. Your tool, the young wolf from the Pack, has escaped unscathed and won't remember anything in the morning. Neither will you." She drew a breath and whispered, "What happens next?"

A groan tore itself out of Menachem's throat, and he screeched his chair away from the table with a strong shove. His head thrashed back and forth.

"Oh, no," murmured Leery. He dropped his coffee mug, the dregs of his drink splattering his trousers, ceramic shards shrapneling across the room.

"What the hell, Oriscoe?" asked Carmichael, dancing back.

In the interview room, Katzen was growling like a rabid dog, spittle foaming at the corners of his mouth. His eyes glowed with an eerie green light.

Leery ripped his tie off and dropped it on the floor as he stepped toward the door. "Get them out of there, Lieu! He's changing!"

Van Helsing disappeared without a word and reappeared between Evie and Dru. "Out, ladies!" she barked.

But it was too late. Katzen exploded to his feet, his hat flying away, his clothes ripping down the seams. A pelt that was more silver than black showed through the rents in the fabric, and fangs pushed his teeth clattering to the floor.

Leery kicked off his new Florsheim loafers half a step from the door, and then changed, bursting from his own clothes faster and more violently than the rabbi. He grasped the doorknob and flung the door open, bouncing it off the wall.

Menachem threw back his head and let loose with an ear-shattering howl. The fur atop his head tried to knit itself into a *yarmulke*, but something interfered with its formation. Some foul process disturbed the pattern. He bared his teeth at Evie, ignoring Van Helsing, and flexed his hands, clattering his claws on the tabletop in a gross parody of Evie's consistent tapping. He bent forward at the waist and snarled, the fur on his head writhing like a bed of insane snakes as it tried to knit into a *yarmulke*, failed, tried again, failed again.

Leery charged into the room, and as Katzen reached back, back, back in preparation of raking his claws through Dru and Evie's faces, he leaped on him from the side. Together, they rolled, barking and snapping at one another, into the far wall, hard enough to split the plasterboard and splinter one of the studs behind it.

"Out!" yelled Van Helsing.

Evie reacted first, shoving herself away from the snarling ball of fangs, claws, and fur, then sprinting for the door. Dru stood with an almost lazy slowness, as though there was nothing out of the ordinary. She sketched runes in the air with each hand, her eyes locked on the struggling wolves.

"Get out of here, Nogan!"

One of the wolves whined and yelped, and Dru stepped closer to the pair, rather than going the other way. She connected seven runes with her left hand and twelve with her right. The rune set on her left glowed a mean, savage purple, and bright electric blue bathed her right side. She uttered a word in the *Verba Patiendi,* and the left-hand runes began to spin around the center of the rune set, accelerating with each twitching spin of her index finger until the runes first became a blur, then disappeared like the teeth on a saw blade. At the same time, the seven-pointed star in the center became a solid disc of midnight purple. She barked a short, barbaric-sounding phrase in the language of suffering and flicked her fingers toward the wolves, following it with her eyes and chanting under her breath. The midnight purple disc burned through the air, leaving the scent of brimstone behind.

Angie Carmichael filled the doorway to the observation room. "Dru!" she yelled, beckoning her. "Let Leery handle it!"

Dru ignored her, gaze riveted to the spinning purple rune set that seemed to suck the light from the room. The air cracked with tiny, midnight purple spheres of ball lightning, and her hair began to stand on end. She held out her left hand and snapped her fingers, then caught her materializing battlestaff, its blood garnets already glowing with hot red light. Her eyes lit up, glowing firetruck red and seeming to suck air from the room like a forge's flames.

"Out, you bricky, mafficking church bell!" Epatha yelled at Dru. She reached for her shoulder but snatched her hand back as though Dru burned at the temperature of the sun. She turned away, holding her translucent hand to her chest, eyes wide.

The spinning disk of malefic energy zipped into the ball of snarling fur and fangs and exploded, shoving Leery away as though with a soft invisible hand, and splattering Rabbi Katzen into the corner as though struck by a battering ram. Leery's gaze snapped around and pinned her where she stood, but she ignored his glare. She flicked the electric blue rune set and spoke a single word in a spidery tongue that sounded a little like Hebrew. As the sound of the word faded, the rune set imploded, leaving behind an electric blue mist. She flicked her fingers again, and the mist raced toward Leery like a weird snake. It circled around him, finding the unhealed cuts beneath his fur and saturating the wounds with blue light.

Menachem whimpered in the corner; his head rocked back and pressed against the door. His eyes were squeezed shut, and blood trickled from one of his ears.

Dru extended her staff toward him, the giant garnet at its top shimmering with internal flames the color of red licorice. Something seemed to dance within that light, something dark and vicious, something pestilent and poisonous.

Leery leaped across the table and batted her staff up and away, growling the way a wolf might growl at a balky pup. Her gaze snapped to his, eyelids narrowing for a moment, and then the baleful red light began to bleed away from both her eyes and the stones set in the ends of her staff.

In the corner, Menachem groaned and slumped into unconsciousness, his body regaining the shape of a doughy old man. Van Helsing darted an appraising glance at Dru over her shoulder, a doubtful expression on her face. "What was that, Nogan?"

Dru looked at her with a bland expression on her face. "That was me containing the situation."

Van Helsing shook her head, then glanced at Katzen's unconscious form. "Go on, Leery. Get changed." She turned and pointed at Dru. "And you. Use one of those healing spells of yours on the suspect here. Then make sure he is clothed and comfortable. I'm making him your responsibility. Get me, Nogan?"

Dru lifted one shoulder and let it drop. "No problem, Lieu."

33

Forty minutes later, Leery entered the interview room carrying two cups of coffee. "The lieu wants you, Dru," he said as he put a cup of coffee in front of Menachem and took the seat across from him.

"Sure," said Dru. She turned and went into the observation room.

"Lerome... What happened?"

"Detectives Evans and Nogan were questioning you. You freaked out, Menachem. Brought out fur and fang."

"No!"

Leery nodded and sipped his coffee. "Yes."

"Ach. My head feels like someone parked the Tank on it."

"That's what happens when you attack the cops, Menachem."

Katzen shook his head and picked up his coffee. "What is happening to me, Leery?"

"That's what we need to find out." Leery sipped his coffee and looked at Menachem askance. "I noticed something about your change."

"You noticed something about my *change*?"

Leery nodded. "Your *yarmulke* wouldn't settle down. It was like something was interfering."

Menachem sniffed. "What?"

"Some black magic, I'd say. Something trying to control you. Something wired to your wolf. Something that protects whoever did this to you."

"That was no dream, was it, Leery?" Katzen asked in a small, unsure voice.

"I don't think it was, Mendel. I don't think you believe it was either."

"I should be so lucky." Menachem sipped his coffee. "I *did*, Leery. Before all this ruckus. I did believe that. I wish I still could."

"I know," said Leery in a subdued voice.

"So. What happens now?"

"First thing, Mendel, is we find the spell that brought out your wolf and disarm it. Then, we figure out who was controlling your mind."

Menachem shook his head and cut his gaze away from Leery's. "And I have to live with this thought of someone being able to call me and make me dance on a string? I must live with this pain?"

"No, Menachem. You don't have to live with that," said Leery in a quiet voice.

"So. You can dispel that, too?"

"I don't need to. If you think about it, Rabbi, you'll know why."

Katzen cocked his head to the side and pursed his lips. "I don't know, Leery."

Leery sighed. "It's something *you* taught *me*, Rabbi. There's always an alternative. Pain only exists because there's an awareness of pain. Let go of that awareness, Menachem. Turn your awareness to God."

"Yes, of course." Katzen raised his eyes to meet Leery's gaze. "And the mind control?"

"No one has power over you, Rabbi, unless you give it to them."

Menachem lifted his chin and let it drop. "It sounds so simple."

"Listen to me, Mendel. I spoke with the man that crafted the spell that's cast on you. He said the key to it was that you had great faith but also a vulnerability."

"Ah." Menachem sipped his coffee, returning his gaze to its rippled surface as he set it down. "I see it now. Regardless of what you tell yourself, Leery, you're not above the occasional mitzvah."

"You understand what the spellcrafter meant?"

"Sure. The one who cast this nightmare on me must be someone I trust. Someone close to me. Someone I'd willingly allow to subsume my will."

"And who is that person, Mendel?"

The rabbi continued to stare at his coffee cup and heaved a sigh. "There are a few, Leery. But only one who worries me."

"His name, Rabbi?"

"My grandson. The one who is searching for the face of God in the gutter. The one who seeks God's grace with a needle in his arm."

Leery said nothing, waiting.

Katzen heaved another sigh, and his shoulders slumped. "Do me another mitzvah, Lerome Oriscoe. Do not allow harm to come to my grandson."

"I'll do what I can, Mendel, but it's not all up to me."

"And so it goes. Lev is his name." He lifted his gaze and pinned Leery with it. "Lev Katzen. His home is in the old neighborhood, but you won't find him there. He is in Mamaroneck, these days, staying with the *toyt eyner*. If he is involved, it's because they have tricked him. Used his need to blind him to what he's doing."

"The zees. Why am I not surprised?" muttered Leery.

34

Leery stepped through the door into the observation room. "You heard it all?"

Angie nodded. "I did."

"Will you charge him?"

Angie dropped her gaze for a moment. "I don't know yet, Leery."

"Come on, Angie. You *heard* him. He's not responsible."

"And if it pans out that way, he's got nothing to fear." She held out her hand. "Pick up Lev Katzen. If what the old man said is true, I won't be inclined to prosecute. That's the best I can do."

Leery wagged his head. "He wouldn't lie about it, counselor."

"I'm sure you're right, Leery." She looked at Van Helsing. "Let's get the CSI people in and get these spells taken care of."

"Right," said Epatha. She disappeared.

"Leery..."

"Yeah?"

"You know his grandson is dirty, and I don't just mean with the drugs. This kind of thing...the depth of this casting..." She shook her head. "I doubt it would work if the caster wasn't fully aware of what he was doing."

Leery drew a deep breath and puffed out his cheeks. "Yeah. Menachem can't bring himself to believe it because Lev is his grandson...his flesh and blood."

"I'm saying this because you have to be prepared. Lev isn't going to come in without a fight. He's going to fight, tooth and nail, for his next fix, for his freedom. He's going to lie, to fight dirty, to cheat, to do whatever he has to in order to stay out of jail. You can't go into this with half your arsenal on the shelf because of a promise you made to an old man."

"I know that, Angie. But at the same time, I don't have to go into it looking for a fight, either."

"No, you don't." She patted him on the arm. "Make sure your partner knows that last part, too."

"Right," Leery said with a grimace.

35

Lev Katzen wasn't hard to find. In fact, his face appeared in so much of the surveillance footage on Mama Rose Marie's house that it almost seemed like he was trying to be seen.

"He's not camera-shy, that's for sure," said Evie.

"No," said Leery. "Have you heard from the Ceebies?"

Evie nodded. "They are sending the shamans."

"Oh! Hear that, Dru? The Covenancy Bureau of Idiots is sending in SERT."

"Great. The SWAT team and them can compare the size of their—"

"*And*," said Evie. "They are setting up a simultaneous raid on Mama Rocha's place out in the LA Locus."

"We'd better get out to Mamaroneck, then," said Dru, standing and getting her coat.

"Hey, Evie, why don't you stay here to liaise with the shamans?"

Evie glanced at Dru, then met Leery's gaze. "Yeah, I could do that. I'll find out when they're staging and meet you there."

"Good idea," said Leery.

36

Leery sat in the driver's seat and cranked the ignition as Dru belted herself in. Leery peeked at her, then put the car in reverse and backed out of his improvised space. "Want some coffee?"

"I'll bet you do," said Dru with a grin.

"Well, I *am* breathing, so, yeah."

They rode for a few minutes in silence, then Dru turned, put her back against the door, and stared at Leery. "I didn't do anything wrong."

He took another peek at her face. "Not so much wrong, Dru, as... Hell, I don't know. Maybe you went a little bit too far."

Dru pistoned her shoulders up and down in the space it took to blink. "I thought the situation merited that use of force."

"Listen, I'm not going to complain that you used your skills on my behalf. Not at all, but I had it pretty much under control, right? So, to the lieu, to Carmichael, it might seem excessive."

Dru shrugged in the same hyper-fast motion as before, never taking her eyes off Leery.

"And you did take me out of it to get at him. And I wasn't hurt. I've had worse shaving."

"Yeah, but he *was* hurting you. And it's my job to ward you from harm, to protect you, to do what I can do so you don't *need* to do what you do. Right? I mean, am I misunderstanding the roles here?"

"No, I wouldn't say that." He stared out the windshield for a moment, then glanced at her. "Look, Nogan... Is there something we need to talk about?"

A small smile peeked from her lips. "About what, Leery?"

"Oh, you know. The Mets. The Knicks." He waved his hand in the air. "Whoever is playing right now." The stop-and-go traffic would have irritated him on any other day, but with Dru sitting next to him, looking at him that way, nothing seemed able to touch his mood. Her eyes sparkled, and she chuckled, and Leery had to admit she was quite fetching, in the late afternoon light.

"What?" she asked, a smile flirting with her lips. "What's so interesting over here?"

"Oh, just waiting for you to tell me which sport is in season and which teams I'm interested in." He flashed his patented Leery-smile (guaranteed to melt hearts or your money back) at her, then forced his gaze to the front.

"Oh, is that all?"

"So... Uh... How are things going with Epatha?"

"With the lieu? Better, as far as I can tell, but she's hard to read."

Leery couldn't be sure, but he thought amusement rippled in her voice. He threw a quick glance at her, and she met it without blinking or turning away. "Yeah, I know all about hard to read." He cleared his throat. "But with Epatha, what you see is pretty much what you get. It's that Victorian Age upbringing, I think."

"Must have been hard."

"What, growing up in the time of Queen Victoria? Except for the prudishness, it seems like a time where the moral majority had things the right way around."

"Well, that, too, but I meant growing up the daughter of the Grand Cynosure of the Covenancy. Talk about expectations."

"Oh, she was already grown before he ascended to the hot seat. For her formative years, old Abe was just your routine paladin."

"'Routine paladin?' No such thing, Leery," she said and let loose with a bell-like laugh. "Abraham Van Helsing was a vampire hunter cum demon slayer. Did you know he was an ordained priest before he met Epatha's mother?"

"No, I didn't. Boy, you really do your research."

More bell-like laughter filled the car. "No, silly. Mommy told me all about them when the lieu and I were having our little disagreements."

"Ah."

"Well, Daddy, too. He wasn't happy I was working with one of 'old Abe's' children."

"I'll bet. Hercule must have had his run-ins with the Van Helsing clan."

"I'm sure he did, but Daddy will never speak to *me* about it. He just says '*Ma chère, ces jours sont terminés.*'"

"Those days are over, eh? Well, you know what they say."

"What's that?" she asked in a mischievous tone.

"Loose lips sink ships." More laughter rang out, and Leery smiled along with it.

"There are other things to do with your lips than sink ships," Dru said.

"Sure, sure. Like drinking coffee, eating vending machine sandwiches, uh...whistling, holding up mustaches..."

"Is that all you can come up with?"

"Hey, it's been a long day."

"Speaking of coffee... Isn't there a Starbucks two blocks up?"

"Yes," he said.

"Then, are you going to make good on your offer to buy me a cup of coffee?"

Leery glanced at his watch. The SWAT team wouldn't be done with their boring planning sessions for another couple of hours, and when the SERT team would arrive was anyone's guess. "Sure. We've got the time."

"Then pull over. I gave up sniffing glue this week, so I could use a blast of caffeine."

"Uh...right." Leery swooped into a six-foot gap between a Honda and an old Chevy and bumped the front tires up on the sidewalk. "This'll do. We won't be long."

Chuckling, Dru got out and allowed him to hold the coffee shop's door open for her.

37

L eery pulled onto Topsail Lane and parked behind the SWAT tractor-trailer. He killed the last of his *trenta* and gestured at the C3 with the empty cup. "Do you suppose they'll have more coffee in there?"

"Bad coffee? Sure. They may be SWAT, but they're still cops."

Leery grimaced and looked inside his empty cup. "I'd like another cup or two, but I don't know if it's worth the risk of getting sucked into their planning session."

"I didn't think they were so bad during the Van Dee case."

"Well, you're still a green detective. When you amass a mountain of experience like I have, planning briefings are a waste of time."

Dru rolled her eyes and turned to look out into the gathering gloom of evening—but not before he saw the telltale signs of her amusement. "You know what's funny?"

"The fact that people think Facebook is a news reporting service?"

She chuckled and turned her gaze back to him. "That, too. But I was going to say that it's funny everyone assumes the succubus they just met is young. I mean, everyone knows a succubus can change her appearance to suit her target's desires."

"To be honest, having met several of your kind these past few months, I'm surprised anyone can think at all in your presence."

"Aw, Leery, you say the sweetest things."

"Sure. I'm good at it. Listen: sugar, cherry snow cones, candy canes, grape pie, cane syrup—"

"Ha-ha, Mr. Comedian."

"But, yeah, you can't blame a guy for taking what he sees at face value. You gals are kind of wired to underscore that a little, aren't you?"

"Uh, 'gals?'"

Leery shrugged. "Girls. Womenses. Female tamales. Whatever."

"The term is succubi, wolfman."

"The term is Adonis-like-example-of-alpha-wolf."

"Meee-yow!" she said with a saucy grin.

Leery looked mournfully down at his empty cup.

"Come on, Mr. Alpha-wolf. I'll go get the coffee for you. You wait outside so I can play the cutesy 'my-partner-sent-me-dimple-dimple' routine and not get trapped inside."

"Sounds like a plan." The two got out, and Leery handed over his Starbucks cup. Dru winked and spun on the balls of her feet, then headed inside. Leery watched her every second until the door cut off his view. "Come on, Oriscoe," he murmured. "You know better than this. Get it out of your head." He turned and walked back toward Van Wagenen Avenue, opening his coat and letting the brisk wind ruffle around inside.

The SWAT team had disabled the streetlights on both Topsail and Van Wagenen, and as the sun set, night fell around him like a rogue wave of black water. He inhaled, drawing the scents of the Mamaroneck neighborhood across his olfactory hairs, trying to assess what he couldn't see in the gloaming. His human senses weren't as good as his wolf form could provide, but they were night-and-day better than an ordinary human's.

He could smell the salt from Long Island Sound a few blocks to the east, as well as the fishy and rotting vegetation odor from the Porgy Shoal off the point. The aromas of impending dinner time drifted on the slight breeze, along with the slimy taste of human body odor and the various tangs of machinery—oil and fuel. Somewhere in the distance, a mother yelled for her child to "get his ass inside before it gets whopped," and he grinned, thinking of countless such calls to dinner his mother had shouted at him.

Behind him, the door set in the side of the C3 trailer banged open, followed by Dru's chuckle and the sound of Evie's voice as she told Dru a story about "the good old days" when she and Leery were partnered up. "Don't believe a word she says, Dru," he said without turning. "She's the biggest liar at 1 PP."

"Shush, *Lerome*," said Evie. "I've never told a lie in my life."

"No, of course not!" said Leery as he turned, a grin decorating his face. The shadows behind the C3 rippled and twitched, and Leery froze, narrowing his eyes and squinting into the gloaming.

"What?" said Dru, glancing in the direction he stared.

"Something in the dark," Leery said. Keeping his eyes locked on the darkness behind the C3, he motioned Dru and Evie to come toward him while stepping out of his Florsheims. "Grab my hat, Dru."

She set his Starbucks cup on the roof of their Crown Victoria and moved toward the back of the car, her gaze zipping back and forth along the trees lining the street. "Sure thing," she said.

Evie walked toward Leery, her gaze locked on his face, but her hand had drifted inside her coat—a subtle move, but one Leery was familiar with. She was a Mesmer, the same as Mesmerina had been. Her magic was limited to mind control techniques, so Evie relied on an artifact for fighting. In a special pocket of her coat, she carried a twelfth-century short bow that had been "blessed" by Pestilence and War at the bequest of Genghis Khan himself, who had named it Nightshade.

Leery slid out of his own coat and let it pool on the ground behind him. He twitched his tie, and the trick-knot he used gave way, letting the tie slide from around his neck.

Dru popped the trunk, using the movement to hide her hands as she sketched a quick rune set. She withdrew Leery's black woolen hat and turned to sail it in his direction. At the same time, she connected six runes the color of a deep bruise with two triangles arranged like the Star of David. As she connected the last triangle, the rune set began to pulse with a slow, deliberate rhythm. As she threw the hat, she flicked the rune set along with it.

After undoing the clasp on his belt, Leery went to work on the buttons of his shirt. He caught the hat and flipped it onto his head with a vaudevillian flourish. Dru's dark rune set settled under the brim, coming to a feathery landing on his forehead.

The shadows pulsed and flickered between the trees once more as though a black sheet hung between the trunks and someone—or *something*—moved behind that dark curtain. Behind their cruiser, Dru slammed the trunk lid and sent a casual glance toward the woods. She picked up the cup of coffee she'd brought out. "Oh! I forgot the cream and sugar!" she called and walked toward the C3 steps. Her left hand hung near her hip, and she wrote runes in the air as she walked, but at a much smaller scale than she usually did to make it less obvious what she was doing.

"Thanks!" Leery called after her. He raised his hands as though stretching, slipping the shirt off his shoulders and letting it fall as he dropped his hands.

"Hey, sexy, wait for me," said Evie. "It's more fun if we undress each other."

"Yeah, Dru can play catch-up when she comes back with the coffee." The rune set on his forehead tingled, and the tingle grew into a mild burning sensation—like the sun beating down on his forehead at Daytona Beach in August.

Dru climbed the steps of the C3 and sent one last, darting glance at Leery. He nodded back to her. "Seven sugars this time!" he yelled.

Dru grasped the knob and turned it, and as she did so, the shadows flickering in the woods solidified into a platoon of shadow people. She dashed inside and slammed the door.

Evie dashed to Leery's side as he stepped out of his trousers and kicked them aside. "Stay behind me," he said. "If they flank, get to the C3 anyway you can. They can't hurt me, so don't worry about that."

As soon as he said it, the closest shadow person grinned—a brilliant bluish gash through the fabric of—and pulled a thirteen-inch silver dagger from behind his back.

"Okay, maybe I was wrong about that, but do it anyway." Leery glanced at Evie, and she nodded as she pulled Nightshade from her coat. It didn't look like much—a straight stick of wood roughly twenty-four inches long. It had no bowstring and didn't need one. Nor arrows. He grinned at her and snap-changed into his wolf form. As the change raced through his body, the rune set on his forehead scorched him and a flame the color of raven feathers erupted across his body. Though black, the flames glowed somehow bright while at the same time seeming to devour the ambient light around him.

Evie lifted Nightshade and mimed pulling back the non-existent bowstring. The shadow people gave a collective hiss as a bowstring and arrow sketched in a poisonous green light appeared. She opened her fingers, and the arrow zipped across the road, hitting the shadow person with the silver dagger in the breastbone, lifting him, and flinging him back toward the trees.

The creature screamed and thrashed, grabbing at the glowing arrow with his free hand, but when his hand passed through it, his shrieks ratcheted up a notch. He lost his grip on the dagger and curled into a fetal position as the arrow continued to snail its way into his flesh.

Leery snarled and leaped to the side of the road, throwing his arms wide and beckoning with his clawed fingers. A sickly-green arrow slid through the air a foot to his right, and another shadow person flew back the way he'd come, hissing and crying out in agony.

But there were plenty of others sprinting, dancing, or leaping out of the woods. Their form was hard to pin down, hard to observe. Composed of shifting, shadowing blackness, they were roughly humanoid, but if Leery looked too long at any one point of their anatomy, that part seemed to liquefy and reform.

Not all of them bore silver armaments—or if they did, they kept them hidden to surprise him with later. Evie fired poisonous arrow after pestilent arrow at a rapid rate: picking a form, drawing the magical bowstring back and letting fly, then repeating the process faster than she could draw a deep breath. A paltry few arrows missed the mark, but for each hit, the shadow person she aimed at was taken out of the fight.

Glowing, ethereal servitor warriors slid through the C3 trailer's metal skin into the dark shadow it cast. They began hacking and slashing a swath toward Leery and Evie with glowing, ethereal melee weapons. As they did, the doors on the street side of the trailer banged open, allowing a flood of therianthropes to charge out, followed by Dru and a few witches. Even with the SWAT team fully deployed, however, they were outnumbered three to one.

The four SWAT therianthropes from the Van Dee case moved as a unit to meet their servitor compatriots already between the C3 and the line of trees. The Ganeshan nodded toward Leery, and the young werewolf howled a greeting. The other SWAT units gathered themselves, and then the units charged as one into the darkness beneath the branches.

Leery threw back his head and howled as he raced toward the undulating darkness in front of him. Behind, Evie continued to fire magical arrows of acidic poison into the swirling murk. The black flames coating Leery's skin flashed and grew as he approached the shadow people rushing to meet him. All of them had drawn a silver weapon—daggers, hatchets, throwing stars, even a giant fork of some kind.

"Leery!" shouted Dru as she rushed out of the C3. She flung a brilliant rune set the orange color of tigers at him. The runes inside the thirteen-pointed star glowed and pulsed as the spell raced toward him.

One of the shadow men sprinted at him, a hatchet waving above his head. Leery swiped at him with his claws, and the coal-black flames surrounding his hand arced out, slapping at the shadow man. A sound like ripping fabric rang out, and the shadow man screeched, his silver hatchet falling through him to bounce on the grass at his feet. The bruise-colored flames wrapped around the creature of darkness, and he shrank and shrank until he disappeared with a faint pop.

Another shadow man skidded to a stop, but a shadow woman hadn't seen the fate of the first, and she came on, dagger held out in front of her like a talisman, an eerie wail accompanying her. When she reached a spot about a yard from Leery, the flames lashed out again, encapsulating the woman. She screamed and thrashed as if aflame, her dagger falling to the ground at her feet.

Leery skidded to a stop and straightened, watching with a horrified expression as the midnight flames consumed the shadow woman. The shadow people stopped advancing toward him and abandoned their humanoid shapes in favor of an ill-defined fog of ebony swirls, some taking their silver weapons with them, but many dropping them in their haste to escape the dark, all-consuming flames.

The orange rune set settled over him, and the ebony flames seemed to drink in the orange glow. Leery's vision brightened, and a feeling of power surged through him. He stepped forward and bent low, scooping up a pair of silver throwing stars conveniently shaped like the Star of David.

He peered at the pool of swirling caliginous forms beneath the trees and could see each individual creature and the silver weapons they carried. The flames surrounding him no longer appeared to be black, but rather seemed to encompass a kaleidoscope of colors in every hue. Fascinated, he held up his hand, and the flame leaped from him to the collective of shadow people in front of him.

The myriad-colored flame slammed into the murky fog like a wave crashing against a rock cliff, sparks of flame and motes of shadow flying away into the night. The flames raced across the surface of the clump of shadow until they covered every surface Leery could see. Inside the sphere of flame, the shadow people writhed in agony. The rainbow sphere sucked the light away from its interior in rapid pulses, and with each pulse, the screaming increased while the shadowy forms shrank.

"Wow," said Evie from beside him. "Your new partner..."

Leery glanced at Evie and nodded.

The multi-colored ball of flame consumed the last of the light inside itself, and with it, the last of the shadow people. The ball collapsed to the size of a marble, then disappeared.

Dru jogged up to them, her gaze skimming over Leery, the worried expression she wore fading as she saw no wounds. She turned her gaze on the dark woods and raised her hand. "There are more." She stepped forward and began another rune set.

Leery looked at Evie, and the woman shrugged, then moved to stand with Dru, raising her bow and firing glowing arrows into the darkness.

In the woods behind the C3, the Garudan shrieked with fury, accompanied by the Ganeshan's bellows, followed by the sound of a tree trunk splintering and toppling into the brush.

Leery charged around Dru and Evie, his head down and forward, bent at the waist to give them clear lines of sight beyond him. His tail was rigid behind him, and his taloned toes dug into the soft soil as he propelled himself toward the cold darkness as fast as he could manage. Dru shouted something that had a lot in common with the harsh ringing of massive bells, and the woods seemed to shudder as though caught in the throes of a violent windstorm.

The remaining shadow people nearby turned and bolted deeper into the shadowed woods, some abandoning their weapons in their haste. Leery slowed as he crossed over the edge of the wood. He glanced left, toward the C3, and saw that all of the creatures of darkness were fleeing. Some of the SWAT officers gave chase, but the majority merely watched.

The air was filled with the murderous basso thump of incoming helicopters, and the downdraft from the circling vehicles washed through the trees. Thick ropes fell from the fuselage of the helo nearest Leery, and eight figures slid out and down the lines to the ground. Each wore a black uniform with a SERT patch on the right shoulder, a CBI patch on the left. They were festooned with fetishes, charms, and geegaws according to his or her specialty.

The group surrounded Leery, and one of them stepped closer. "Freeze right there, wolf!" she commanded. She leveled a totemic wand capped by a grinning skull at him.

"Ho, there!" shouted Dru. "He's a cop."

The shaman glanced at Dru and gave her a little eye-pop, then tore her gaze back to Leery. She straightened and dropped her wand into a sheath at her right hip. "Sorry," she said. "Our briefing was a little thin on account of the shadow people raid."

Leery nodded and gestured deeper into the woods.

"Right," said the leader of the SERT unit. "I'm Fanny Blackfire, Covenancy Bureau of Inquisition, SERT division."

"I'm Dru Nogan, this is Detective Yvonne Evans, and the wolf is Detective Leery Oriscoe."

Fanny cocked her head to the side and looked up at Leery, eyes sparkling. "Oriscoe, huh? I've heard of you."

A soft growl rumbled in Leery's chest.

"The shadows are getting away," said Dru. "And the real targets of this raid will no doubt now know we are here. Can I suggest we get moving?"

"We'll need to liaise with your SWAT commander first. We'll be ready in thirty minutes or so."

With a louder growl, Leery shoved Blackfire aside and raced into the woods, moving through the brush with that utter silence only werewolves seemed capable of.

Behind him, he heard Dru say, "Do that if you want, but you're going to miss the raid."

"What? I... No, you misunderstand me. We can't—"

"See you when we get back then. SWAT's already deployed and giving chase to the shadow people. I'm sure the local branch of *Noster Est* sent shadows as a distraction to cover their escape."

Leery quit listening to what went on behind him and gave his full attention to the trees and brush between him and Van Dee's McMansion. To his left and right, he heard the therianthropes from SWAT keeping pace. His gaze zipped from one pool of shadows to the next, but he saw no more shadow people.

He came to a stop a yard or so from the edge of the estate's lawn and crouched. As with every time he'd visited, the house was lit up like a whorehouse on a dark winter night, and the drive was filled with vehicles. Unlike the other visits, however, black cloth covered all the floor to ceiling windows.

"They hung those about an hour ago," a voice whispered from the brush to his right. Leery whirled that direction, claws out. "Relax, Leery. It's Epatha."

Leery cocked his head to the side in the manner of every canine confronted with something he doesn't understand.

Van Helsing chuckled. "I haven't lost *all* my street chops. You can stop gawking. Who better to play advance scout than a ghost?"

He nodded and turned back to the house, then shook his head.

"Wait here. I'll head in and check it out," said Van Helsing.

Leery shook his head, but it was too late, Van Helsing had disappeared. He took a single step toward the house, but the only thing he could think of more reckless than a single cop—ghost or not—heading inside was another cop following her.

Almost invisible in the darkness, five servitor warriors slid into the lawn from the line of trees. They'd muted their incandescence somehow, and their nature dictated they float a few inches off the ground, making no sound. They moved forward, hunched at the waist, and stopped against the glass walls of Van Dee's house. One of them held up a finger and stuck his head inside. A roar like that of a freight train moving at top speed came from within the house, and the servitor jerked his head back through the glass wall and signaled his companions to get ready.

Back in the woods, Leery crouched in a sprinter's pose as Dru and Evie came up behind him, followed by the SERT unit.

"This is reckless!" hissed Fanny Blackfire.

"You don't have to come," said Dru in a bored-sounding voice.

Leery twisted around and glared at them, making a throat-slitting gesture. Dru winked at him and came to stand at his side. Evie took the other flank, still holding Nightshade, and the SERT unit members arrayed themselves in a skirmish line beyond her.

The basso growl from within the house intensified to ear-splitting levels, and the glass walls shattered into the lawn. The servitors began wielding magic, large swaths of glowing power sheeting into the house from their fingertips. With bellows that would sound right at home at any big zoo, their therianthrope team members charged out of the woods, forming wedges or attack lines near their servitor warriors.

Tenebrous waves of magic the color of spent motor oil poured out of the smashed windows, killing the shrubs, flowers, and grass within ten feet of the house. The servitors waded into the mix, dispelling what they could, trying to turn the rest harmlessly into the sky. As that first wave of power faded, the therianthropes roared again and charged inside, the black curtains blowing in the wind of their passage.

Leery bolted forward, followed by Dru and Evie. After a moment, the SERT unit also came out of the woods, each member holding a charm, a totemic wand, a generic effigy, or a gris-gris.

Unseen behind them, Van Helsing appeared on her knees, clutching her head.

Leery charged into the house, feeling the tingling mantle of one of Dru's protective wards settling around him. He ripped the black cloth down and dropped it on the floor. He caught sight of Van Helsing and pointed at her, waving to catch Dru's attention.

She whirled and yelled, "Healer!" Then, she raised her own hand to point at the lieutenant. "Get a healer over there!"

Leery whirled away, sprinting deeper into the house, following the therianthropes. The SWAT teams formed a skirmish line as horde after horde of zees poured up from the basement, but he didn't slow and join them—he kept his gaze focused on the door that led out of the big room.

The door disintegrated in a furious wash of foul black power, and time seemed to slow to a molasses-crawl. Leery hurled himself to the side, seeming to fall in slow motion as flame first blossomed, then gouted through the doorway. He hit the ground and rolled, trying to clear the line of attack from the hall beyond that door—and the tall woman standing there readying her next spell.

Karma. For a moment, her gaze locked on his, then she lifted it away and hurled a wad of murk toward the SWAT units fighting the zombies behind Leery.

He sprang to his feet, snarling, and flung one of the silver Stars of David he'd liberated from the shadow people. It sailed toward Karma, glistening in the incandescent light from the servitor warrior's spells, and Leery loped behind it. If he could get close enough to spring on her, he could probably keep her from casting the next spell. *Probably.*

If he couldn't, there was no doubt who her next target would be.

Behind him, the *whump* of large-scale magical ordinance shook the house, followed by the splattering rain of zombie body parts falling from where they'd smacked into the ceiling. Karma's gaze flicked toward him, and she sneered as she twisted to face him. She slashed her hand through the air, and the silver shuriken was slammed aside to clatter harmlessly on the floor. She brought both hands toward him, fingers extended, and began to chant in a patois that sounded bayou to Leery's Bronx ears. Energy began to gather between her palms, small arcs of greenish-blue lightning arcing between her fingertips.

He flung the other throwing star without pausing, hoping to distract her for at least a moment. *Almost close enough. Almost there.* He couldn't help hunching lower to the ground as her chanting neared crescendo. Her pupils dilated from the power she was calling forth. Her eyes widened, going very round and showing sclera all the way around as the shuriken drew closer and closer. At the last moment, she jerked her torso sideways, and the star passed within a quarter of an inch from her neck. She kept her focus despite it, and the power she was accumulating continued to grow.

As Leery launched himself into the air, going flat with his arms thrown in front of him like a star receiver going for an overthrown pass, a glowing green arrow snaked past him. Karma's eyes went wider yet, and she threw herself to the side, the magic she'd been gathering exploding into the ceiling instead of Leery's face. Dru screamed his name, and then he was on Karma, snapping and clawing while she flung weak magic in his face.

She brought her knee up toward his crotch, but Leery turned it aside, planting his own knee in the middle of her thigh and bearing down. Karma flung herself to the side, but Leery outweighed her by more than two hundred pounds, and he used every ounce of it to keep her pinned beneath him. He snarled at her as she began to chant, then stretched his jaws wide and dropped his face toward her neck.

"Okay! Okay, you fucking mutt! I surrender!"

He kept going until his fangs brushed against her flesh, and then he stopped and snarled his best snarl.

"I said, I give up!"

Leery lifted his head and glowered down at her for a long moment, then shifted his weight back, resting on his heels with his hands still on her shoulders, ready for anything. Behind him, the fighting was dying down as the last of the zees from the basement came upstairs and saw the battle was lost.

Dizziness swarmed around Leery as if he were drunk, and he shook his head to clear it. It didn't help, and instead, a greasy queasiness belched up from his stomach. The urge to close his eyes, to find a dark corner, and to sleep, came over him.

38

Dru saw the glimmer of something settle over Leery like a shroud, and she gasped. Moving on autopilot, her hands started sketching runes in the air, even as she started running.

But she knew it was too late for another ward. Whatever spell was being cast on him, it had already landed.

39

Leery heard Dru gasp and run toward him, but he found it hard to care. A low susurration, a harsh murmur, filled his ears. He could almost make out words in the noise, but no matter how much he strained, he couldn't resolve them.

Beneath him, Karma's face distorted with an evil, hate-filled grin. "Suck on that, you bastard."

Dru raced past him, sprinting toward the corridor, and the instinct to chase her, to pounce on her before she got out of range, nearly overpowered him.

40

Dru hurled herself into the darkened hallway where nothing moved, and no sound reached her ears. Doors branched off to the left and right, yawning maws of darkness. Her heart thundered in her ears, and she stopped near the first door, then peeked around the corner into the room.

The *empty* room.

A low murmur, like someone praying, reached her from down the hall, and she followed the sound, moving faster and faster as the volume increased.

She lurched into the last room on the left, two rune sets ready to be empowered, her fingers ready to flick the spells where they needed to go. A man in black sat slumped at a table in the center of the room, his head sandwiched in his hands. He was murmuring a constant chain of words in old, Semitic languages.

"Stop!" she yelled, and then she powered one of her rune sets with a guttural bark in the language of suffering. She flung the silver rune set at him, and her fingers danced over the other set, making subtle modifications here and there. "Stop your spell, or this next one will burn you to the core!"

The man swiveled in his chair, and he glared at her, but his lips never stopped moving.

"Your funeral," she said with a shrug. She screeched a word in the *Verba Patiendi* and stirred the air with her finger. As she drew back her arm to hurl the spell, a furred fist caught her hand and held it.

41

In Leery's eyes, the world spun and danced, stabbing at him with spears of brilliance and effulgence. The sounds of the house hammered at his eardrums and churned in his stomach. It was worse than any carnival ride he'd ever had the displeasure of riding. He staggered through the door, and Dru said something or other that he couldn't parse. She drew back her hand, and he moved without thinking, grabbing her wrist and holding it.

Sitting at a table in the middle of the room was a man who bore a striking resemblance to

Menachem Katzen, though younger and though wearing all black, not dressed as a Hassid. His eyes narrowed, but his continually moving lips spread in a derisive smile.

Leery couldn't understand what he was saying any more than he could understand Dru's speech a moment before. But, he could understand Lev's triumphant expression without any difficulty.

Smiling, Lev barked something, but when Leery didn't move, his smile began to fade. Eyes burning with anger, he repeated the phrase and flicked an angry, savage gesture at Dru.

Leery felt hot bile in the back of his throat, and the roaring in his ears intensified. He still held Dru by the wrist, but his grip slackened, and she jerked her hand free. She treated him to a brief, but intense, stare, then swept away the rune set she'd been working on and began another one.

Lev lurched to his feet and pointed an index finger at Dru, shaking with the intensity of his anger and hate. He stomped his foot.

Leery's head seemed ready to split, and his guts felt like he'd eaten Hot Pockets for lunch. He twisted his gaze back and forth between

Dru and Lev, no longer quite sure what he'd been about to do.

Dru finished a simple rune set and connected the runes in a six-pointed star. She said something that made Leery burp sharp acid into his mouth, then flung the cherry red runes at Lev.

Lines of brilliant red descended on Lev, wrapping him tight like the webbing of a candy spider, and the man screamed in anger. He tried to lurch away, but Dru's spell had already weakened him to the point that bearing his own weight was too much of an effort. He dropped to his knees, and his lips slowed to a stop, his dark eyes boring into Leery as though his will, alone, could make the werewolf act.

Almost immediately, the sharp, acidic burning in Leery's throat and mouth receded, and the cotton-headed feeling cleared. He staggered a step and regained his human form. His thinking cleared, and sounds returned to normal volumes. Instead of bright, garish light, he realized the room was dim, shadowed, and none of it hurt his eyes. "Cripes," he croaked. "What the hell was that?"

Dru examined him with an intense gaze. Finally, she nodded. "I'd say you just got a dose of Pierre's domination spell."

"He should go into another line of work. I was more inclined to up-chuck than anything else."

"You fought it. Subconsciously, maybe, but you fought it. That's why you felt so bad. Your stubborn nature saved you from becoming Lev's puppet."

Now supine between them, Lev could do no more than groan.

42

Body wrapped in a blanket of thick wool, his mind wrapped in a blanket of foggy thoughts, Leery walked toward the ambulances, trying not to stumble like a drunk. Evie walked at his elbow, Nightshade hidden in her coat once more, as Dru was babysitting Lev Katzen until the transport vans returned from shuttling zombies to Rikers.

As they approached the row of red and white emergency vehicles, Leery spotted Van Helsing lying on one of the gurneys—well, truth to be told, she hadn't gotten the height quite right, so it appeared the gurney was embedded in her ethereal back.

"Lieu?" he called. "Epatha, are you hurt?"

She lifted her head with a groan and shook it. "Zigged when I should have zagged, and Karma caught up to me."

Leery stopped dead in his tracks. "Lieu? Did you just make a pun?"

Van Helsing sniffed and dropped her head. "I *do* have a sense of humor, Oriscoe. It's just that most of *your* little jokes are a bit lacking in comedic value."

A smile danced on Leery's lips, and he hitched his shoulders. "Everyone's a critic."

"Tell me you got that bitch."

"I got her, Lieu."

"And the rabbi's grandson?"

"Dru's got him under control. Waiting on a transport back to the Two-seven. Should we bring Karma, too?"

"She won't interrogate herself, wolf-breath."

At his elbow, Evie chuckled. "I think the lieutenant has had a bit of pain relief."

"For phantom pain, probably."

"I can hear you both, and I'm not so far gone that I won't remember this."

"Uh, right. Got room for a naked guy in a black woolen hat?"

"Pull up a gurney. We'll carpool to the healer's place."

"I'll go put my thumb on Karma and make sure she goes with Lev," said Evie.

"You do that, Mesmerina," said Van Helsing.

Leery froze mid-step for a tick but plastered a smile on his face and jerked his head at Evie. "Go on, Evie. She's had a rough time of it."

"I'm already gone." She turned and walked back toward the house.

Leery climbed into the back of the ambulance and sat on a padded, yet hard seat opposite the gurney. "I'm going to count this as a win, Lieu. We had a few casualties—you included—but nothing serious, and we not only got Karma and Lev but every single zee in the place."

"'S good, Leery."

"We don't have all the identifications done, yet, but I'd say about a quarter of those zees aren't from this locus. So far, we know we have a few from Chicago, and at least a handful from Los Angeles. I'm willing to bet Vegas is represented in that mess."

"Don't forget Detroit. E'ryone always forgets the Motor City."

"Yes, I'm sure Detroit came to the party, along with Toronto, Philly, and Cibola."

"*Ebola*?"

Leery chuckled. "No, Lieu. Cibola, New Mexico. You know, one of the seven cities of gold."

"Oh. Right. I didn't know they had zombies out there."

"Doesn't everyone?"

"Guess you're right. I ne'er unnerstood the desire, to be frank. Why not give up all the stinking flesh?"

"I don't know, Lieu. I'm kind of attached to mine."

"Yeah. Guess so, but all that eating and drinking and *gas*. Plus, nose hair."

"Gee, Lieu, you paint such pretty pictures when you're stoned out of your gourd."

"I'll have you know specters can't *get* stoned. Not even a little. This is just... This..." She turned her head to look at him. "What was I saying?"

"Nothing, Lieu. Not a thing."

"Oh. Good. That shaman gave me a zap, and my mind is all arfarfan'arf."

"Yeah, I gathered that, Epatha. It's okay. You'll feel better after the healer has a look."

"Butter upon bacon, if you ask me. I'm fine as wine, and twice as yummy."

"Righto, Lieu. Why not take a little nap?"

"Well, the dustman is pulling at my peepers."

"Whatever you say, Epatha. Close those little eyes and have a sleep."

"Doesn't do me any good to close my eyes, Oriscoe. I can see through my eyelids."

CHAPTER 3

THE COURT CASE

I

Sam McCoy plodded into the squad room, his wet overcoat draped over his arm, his hair sleep-tossed, and his eyes red. "This had better be good, Oriscoe."

"Well, hello, *Angie*. You don't look so good. In fact, you sort of look like a bitter old man."

"Very funny. Tell me why I'm here."

"Remember Shondra Becker?"

"Karma Becker?"

"The very one."

"Of course, I remember her."

Leery smiled and jerked his chin at the observation room. "She's in the box."

McCoy lifted his eyebrows. "Yes? On what charge?"

"You're going to love this. We've got Karma on twenty counts of assault on a law enforcement officer, thirteen counts of battery on a LEO, two counts of conspiracy to commit magical murder in the first, using mind magic without a license, conspiracy to commit psychic assault in the first degree."

"And her co-conspirators? Who are they?"

"A kid named Lev Katzen. We've got him in holding. And the LA sheriff's office has Mama Aida Rocha in their tank."

"TICO?"

"You bet, with Karma as a co-defendant."

A slow, predatory grin spread across McCoy's face. "That's good, Oriscoe. Good work all around."

"Thanks, Counselor. We held off talking to Karma. I figured you'd want to swing your hammer at her—and to be honest, you'll probably have more success than I would."

"So, is she still pissed about you kicking her ass in LA after the thing with Mesmerina?"

"She hasn't said so, but she did try to cook me about an hour ago."

"Well, I want you in the box with me, then. You play bad cop. I've heard you're sort of good at it." A mischievous grin spread across McCoy's face.

"Sort of? I think I'm offended." He put his hand on McCoy's shoulder. "When you want me to bare my fangs, just say so."

"So." McCoy chuckled. "I want you on her case from the second we walk in there."

"I can do that. Want me to wear my fur coat?"

"And miss out on your witty repartee? No, but feel free to growl."

"That, I can do."

The two entered the interview room by way of the observation room where Dru and Evie stood watching. Leery went in first, wrinkling his nose and showing his teeth at Karma.

"I'd call you 'Akela,' but somehow that sort of seems like a compliment."

"You could always use 'Maugrim,' but I'll tell you, Becker... I've been called worse by better women than you. Nothing you say to me is going to make me tear up."

"Yeah, well. How about I call you 'asshole' and be done with it."

"Suits me. Then I won't feel bad about calling you 'bi—'"

"Shondra Becker, you are in a world of shit," said McCoy, sinking into the chair across from her.

"And who the hell are you supposed to be."

"I'm either your savior or the man who'll chain you to the stake. Sam McCoy is the name."

"Ah," she said with a smile. "The Stakeman, himself. Who knew I rated this much attention on the first interview?"

Standing behind Sam, Leery growled.

"That's cute, asshole," Karma said, cutting her gaze toward him for a moment, then returning it to McCoy. "So, tell me, Sam. What's your offer?"

"My offer?" Sam leaned back in his chair and smiled. "How about we don't try to burn you at the stake? You've earned that, you know."

Shondra scoffed. "Maybe, maybe not. What I know for sure is that this locus no longer allows burnings."

McCoy shrugged. "I can change that."

She narrowed her eyes at him for a moment. "I believe you could, but I don't think you will."

"No? And why's that?"

She tossed her head. "I don't really know. I sense you aren't that eager to prosecute me. I sense that you want my help."

"There are other defendants," McCoy said. "Dozens of them, including Lev Katzen?"

Karma laughed, long and loud. "That patsy?" she chortled. "Sure. Go talk to him."

"Maybe I will."

"While you do, remind him that even if we make a deal with you, that the Covenancy is no doubt standing in the shadows waiting for you to be finished with us. Remind him that no matter what the Locus of New York wants to do to us, a Covenancy dungeon is where we'll end up if *Noster Est* lets us live."

Sam allowed a half-grin to shine for a moment. "Sure. Those are all good reasons for Katzen to deal with me. Haven't you heard? I got a Covenancy deal squashed the last time I had a case against the Zombie mafia."

Shondra tilted her head back, narrowing her eyes and gazing at McCoy with cold calm for the space of a few breaths. "You did that?"

"Sure he did," said Leery. "And Rose Marie Van Dee is in the care of the Locus of New York's corrections department rather than some schmaltzy Covenancy facility. No witness protection. No deal. No chance of getting out for a long, long time."

"That's right," said Sam. "I got her four consecutive lifetimes. And I didn't have evidence half as good as what I have on you."

Karma squinted across the table at him, her nostrils flaring as she breathed. "Idle threats."

"You think so?" Sam turned and glanced back at Leery. "Detective Oriscoe, have you ever known me to make threats I didn't intend to back up?"

"Never," said Leery.

Shondra chuckled sourly. "You know who else I've never seen make a threat she didn't intend to back up with extreme prejudice? Aida Rocha." She shook her head. "No. I don't think I care to deal with the likes of you."

"You rather spend hundreds of years in prison?"

"What I would rather do is not have my immortality challenged by *Noster Est*. Incarceration is nothing. Time in the depths of some stupid dungeon is nothing. Not compared to having my soul shredded by one of Aida's pets." She shook her head again. "Besides, the magister Aida will hire for me could get Ted Bundy acquitted. No. It was a good attempt, Mr. McCoy, but I'm in *no way* interested in your deals. You're wasting time—both yours and mine."

"Fine," said McCoy with a shrug. "I guess we'll see whose vision of the future is more accurate."

"I guess so," said Karma, leaning back in her chair and smiling up at Leery. "You, wolfman, I'll be seeing again."

"Anytime, witch. Any old time at all."

2

Leery had Lev Katzen brought in next and arranged for Becker's transportation to a warded cell in the dungeon beneath Rikers Island. Lev wore a disdainful, self-assured expression that both Sam and Leery saw through at first glance.

"You're going to put your grandfather through all this?" Leery asked. "Shame on you."

Lev turned his face aside, but not before Oriscoe and McCoy saw his stricken expression.

"That's right," said Sam. "It looks like I'll have to charge Menachem. Not enough evidence without him."

"That's too bad," said Leery. "He's guilty as sin, and we have an eyewitness to the murder—the victim, herself." He crossed his arms. "How long do you think he'll get, Sam?"

Sam narrowed his eyes at Lev. "Oh, I'll push for at least five lifetimes. Magical murder in the first, two counts. Using mind magic without a license. I can make those charges stick, and I can make sure we get the right judge."

"Is that what you want, Lev? To send an old man to rot in the dungeon cell next to yours? To betray a man who loves you so much he made me promise to protect you, despite everything you've done to him? To send your grandfather, *the rabbi*, to a dank place full of criminals and killers?"

"Rabbi? He's a werewolf."

"So am I, kid. Is that supposed to mean something?"

"How can you call him a rabbi? The Torah—"

"Listen, kid. You ever hear of King Nebuchadnezzar? How about the tribe of Benjamin?"

Lev shook his head.

"Listen, leaving the dogma aside, I think I can help you, Mr. Katzen," said Sam. "We don't much care about putting you in a deep, dark hole." Sam smiled, and it could have frosted glass. "Don't get me wrong. I'll bury you. *If* you make me. But I'd rather expend my effort on the people that used you for their own ends."

"No one used me!" snapped Lev. "I used *them*!"

"Sure, kid. Sure," said Leery. "Whatever you need to tell yourself. But what Mr. McCoy is offering you is a way to decrease the amount of time you'll spend underground."

"Yeah? At what price?"

"All we want is to get the people at the top of the pile," said McCoy. "People like Aida Rocha in Los Angeles. People like Karma Becker."

"Hah! You want me to trade decades in the dark for eternity? This I need like a hole in the head."

"Your gramps likes that phrase, too, kid," said Leery. "Does he need a hole in the head? Will that finally make you happy? To bring the man down with you?"

"Feh!" Lev crossed his arms. He was pale and clammy, and sweat gathered on his brow.

"What's the matter, Mr. Katzen?" asked Sam with a knowing smile. "Are you feeling under the weather?"

"Now that you mention it, yes, I am. I need my medicine."

"*Medicine!*" Leery barked. "That's what you need like a hole in the head. That junk has ruined your life, kid. Can't you see that?"

"Quit calling me 'kid,'" Lev murmured.

"Let us help you, Mr. Katzen. I can talk to the judge on your behalf. I can get you into a treatment program."

Katzen shook his head and frowned.

"Don't throw everything away for these people, Mr. Katzen. I assure you that they would not do the same for you."

"And how will you keep me alive?"

"Let me tell you, Lev," said Leery. "A month ago, we protected two zees until they could testify against Mama Rose Marie, herself. Want to know where they are right now?"

"Sure," said Lev with a one-shouldered shrug.

"So would I," said Leery. "But the truth is, no one outside the Covenancy Marshals knows where they are. *Who* they are. They got new lives, Lev. New identities."

"And you would do the same for me?"

Leery glanced at McCoy, and Sam nodded. "It's open for discussion."

Lev dropped his gaze to the stained linoleum between his feet. "And Opa?"

"I think we can dispense with any charges against him," said Sam. "*If* you help us get the people we want, I have no need for his testimony, and therefore, no real need to charge him for *your* crimes."

"I really should have a magister," murmured Lev.

"Menachem talked to me without one," said Leery. "Of course, you can have one if you want, but he won't get you a better deal than this."

McCoy nodded. "There is no better deal than this, Mr. Katzen. I promise you that."

Lev ran his hand over his eyes and nodded.

3

Angie smiled as McCoy entered the conference room. Her color was getting back to normal at last, and Sam could barely spot the exhaustion lines around her eyes. She sat on one side of the oak table, and Verbius sat across from her, wearing a sour expression.

"Hello, Verbius," said Sam.

"McCoy," grunted Verbius. "What is it you want now?"

"I know, Verbius. That last case went against you, but I had to do it in the interest of justice. Let me make it up to you."

"Make it up to me, McCoy? Do you know what you cost me? Do you know how incompetent you made me look?"

"I'm sorry for those things, Verbius. Truly. But I've got a gift-wrapped case for you, and I'll help you get it transferred to Covenancy court."

"Is that so? And who is the defendant?"

"Aida Rocha."

Verbius chuckled through a sneer. "Why waste my time with this pretense? Rocha's under arrest in the Locus of Los Angeles. My compatriot out there has her on TICO charges, and, from what I hear, they will get a conviction."

"Sure. All that's true...*if* you let them prosecute her."

"And why wouldn't I?" Verbius scoffed. "She's a resident of LA, McCoy. *They* caught her."

"For TICO, which is a *Covenancy* charge."

"Yes, we've established that."

"It can be tried anywhere. In the Locus of New York, for instance. Wouldn't you rather prosecute? Wouldn't that be a nice feather in your cap?"

Verbius glanced at Angie, noting her smile. "What are you talking about, Sam? Speak plainly."

Sam lifted his chin and grinned. "Verbius, *we* have her cold. I have a witness willing to testify against her. I have her number one enforcer on ice."

"Karma Becker is here? You've arrested her?"

"You bet." Sam paused, eyes twinkling. "And she's been busy in the Locus of New York. Busy on behalf of Mama Rocha."

Verbius looked down at the gleaming tabletop and said nothing for almost three minutes. "Yes," he said. "I want her."

"I thought you might."

"Will Karma testify?"

"No, she's not interested, but we have a co-conspirator who will testify against Karma, and if Karma goes, Aida Rocha goes, too."

"Let's do it."

4

The bailiff heaved a sigh as he watched Sam McCoy and Verbius join Angie Carmichael at the prosecutor's arraignment table. With a small shake of his head, he muttered a curse into his beard and stepped forward. "All rise!" he boomed. "This court is now in session, the Honorable Edgar Cayce presiding."

His Honor, Judge Cayce, floated through the door to his chambers and glided up to the bench. "You may be seated," he said. He glared at the gavel for a moment, then said, "Bang! Let that serve instead of me struggling with this cursed gavel." He turned his gaze on the prosecution table, and his eyes twinkled. "My, my. The courtroom is crowded this morning. An assistant locus magister *and* the executive assistant locus magister. And is that the esteemed Verbius I see? To what do I owe this unexpected pleasure?"

Verbius nodded to the judge and stepped forward. "Your Honor. The Covenancy respectfully asserts jurisdiction in the matter before you."

Cayce frowned and glanced down at his desktop. "But, sir, there is nothing before the Court as of yet."

"No, Your Honor. The first case on your docket, The People versus Shondra Becker, a.k.a. Karma Becker, is the case I'm referring to."

Cayce grunted and flicked his gaze to McCoy. "And I assume the executive assistant locus magister is here to start another war with the Covenancy?"

"No, Your Honor," said McCoy. "I'm here in the interest of justice. Judge Cayce, the Locus Magister's office for the Locus of New York formally supports the Covenancy's assertion of jurisdiction in the matter."

"Curious," muttered Cayce. "Why would you do that, Mr. McCoy?"

"As I said, Judge. In the interest of justice."

Cayce turned to the bailiff. "Bring the accused before me, Wesley."

"Yes, Your Honor." The bailiff turned his head and nodded at Sig Shatenstein, who sat just beyond the bar. Then he turned and waved for another bailiff to fetch Becker from the holding cell.

Once Shondra was standing next to Shatenstein, Cayce turned his attention to her. "Ms. Becker, is it? The Covenancy Magister for the Southern District of the Locus of New York asserts jurisdiction in your case. This means that—"

"Excuse me, Your Honor," said Karma. "But I'm aware of what it means. I have instructed Mr. Shatenstein to assist the Court in any way necessary."

Cayce frowned and lifted an eyebrow. "You have no objections? You do know that Covenancy law can apply more significant penalties for some of the crimes you've been charged with?"

"Yes, Your Honor."

"Mr. Shatenstein?"

"Your Honor, I have instructed my client on this matter and have begged her to fight the transfer, but she is resolute." Shatenstein shrugged.

Cayce twisted his face back and forth between the prosecutors and the defense for a moment. "So be it," he said. "I transfer this case to Covenancy Court for arraignment. Bang!" He flashed a grin at the courtroom, then he disappeared.

6

The wooden-faced bailiff rapped the butt of his spear against the marble cobbles surrounding the bench in the Covenacy courtroom. The galley was packed with onlookers, and the bailiff had to thump his weapon multiple times before silence descended. He glared at the members of the public seated in the benches beyond the bar, then cleared his throat and called, "All rise! The Honorable and Just Samuel Sewall presides over this court! Rise and do him honor!" He knocked his spear against the cobbles one more time.

Judge Sewall didn't do anything as pedestrian as 'make an entrance.' No, he just appeared seated behind the bench, his ghostly hand already extended toward his gavel. He swept it up without so much as a single glare at the thing and banged it against the sound block. "I declare this examination of fact in session! You may regain your seats, though I have been watching this courtroom for many minutes, and I wish to caution those seated beyond the bar. I shall brook no interference in these proceedings, ladies and gentlemen. Upon the cessation of these proceedings due to your actions, I shall become most cross. I hesitate to guess at what I might do, but let it be said I've no compunction to reinstating the stocks and pillory. In my opinion, such things help to ensure public decency. Now..." He broke off as his gaze traveled lazily to the prosecution table. "What's this? What's this? Do my eyes deceive me, or is that esteemed magister, Samuel McCoy, at the People's table?"

"Hello, Your Honor," said Sam.

"It's good to see you, sir, though I must admit my extreme surprise. I believe your last appearance in these vaunted halls was to oppose the man standing at your side? I believe Rhea Dubativo mentioned something of the sort when last we conversed."

"Yes, Judge, but those matters are in the past and were resolved in any case."

"I see, I see." Sewall turned his gaze on Verbius. "Hale, Verbius. You look of good health."

"I am, Your Honor. Thank you for your kind words on the occasion of my hospitalization. I am healed and fit for duty."

"I've no doubt, sir, no doubt." Sewall glanced down at the papers strewn about his desk. "I have it here somewhere," he muttered. "Oh, yes! I take it Mr. McCoy is here to assure the court that there will be no more, *ahem*, disagreements concerning the dispensation of justice in the Southern District of the Great Locus of New York?"

"Well, I can't promise never to disagree with Verbius, Your Honor, but I am here to say that in this case, and in the interest of justice, both within the Locus of New York and without, my beliefs and those of Verbius align. The Locus Magister's office will not oppose these proceedings, Your Honor. In fact, we will be serving in a support role for the Southern District magister as he requires."

"Indeed? Indeed? Oh, that's lovely to see you two fighting side-by-side." He looked down at his papers again. "And I see we have a signed extradition order for one Aida Rocha." He lifted his gaze and found his bailiff. "Is the prisoner ready to be examined?"

"Uh, she is ready for court, Your Honor."

"Yes, yes," said Sewall, seeming somewhat sad. "These things would have been easier back in my day. And the other defendant? This Becker woman?"

"Also present and ready, Your Honor."

Sewall nodded and produced a corncob pipe. "Then, by all means, let us begin."

7

Three days later, Verbius and Sam sat at one of the best tables in the West Room at Vaucluse on East 63rd Street. Verbius forked a bite of his rabbit and reblochon cheese ravioli into his mouth, then smiled at Sam. "You should expand your palate, Sam. These Epaulettes are ridiculously good."

"Thanks, but I'll stick with this New York Strip every time. I'm a meat-eater."

"Yes, but there is rabbit in my dish."

"Rabbit doesn't count as meat, Verbius."

"Oh, but I beg to differ, my friend. I—"

The garçon approached their table, followed by Leery Oriscoe, who wore a pleasant expression everywhere but in his eyes. "I beg your pardon, *Monsieurs*, but this...*gentlemen*"—he gave a sniff and frowned at Leery—"positively insisted we interrupt your repast."

"It's okay, Marcelle," said Verbius. "We know Mr. Oriscoe quite well."

"Yes. I'll leave you to it, then."

"Thank you, Marcelle." Verbius turned his gaze on Leery and arched an eyebrow.

"Yeah. So, there's been a problem at Rikers."

Sam frowned. "Karma?"

"She's fine. Her three attackers aren't so lucky."

Verbius arched a single eyebrow.

"Evidently, Karma is a Sun Tsu enthusiast and thought it was silly to rely on her magic. She's been studying Krav Maga for about twenty years, and she kept it a secret from the zees. There'll be a run on replacement limbs at Rikers, you watch and see."

Sam put his fork down on his plate. "Leery," he began quietly. "Why are you here?"

"Despite how easily she dealt with the attack, it shook Karma up. Shatenstein called the LM's office, and Angie called me to find you. Karma wants to talk."

Sam turned his gaze on Verbius and lifted an eyebrow.

"We're killing them in the courtroom," said Verbius as he gazed mournfully at his Epaulettes. "And I'm really enjoying the dinner."

"It's your case, Verbius, but don't make a rash decision. Think about the information she may have. Yes, we have Rocha on the ropes, but what are the chances Karma can give us one of the other *Noster Est* leaders? I'm sure Rocha loaned out her pet assassin."

Verbius sighed and put down his fork. "Fine. Let's go talk to them. I'm assuming they are at Rikers?"

Leery nodded. "I've got a car outside."

"Oh Lord," murmured Sam. "And we've just eaten."

"What? I'm a *good* driver."

"Uh. Sure. Whatever you say, Oriscoe."

8

Sam, Verbius, and Leery filed into the conference room at Rikers and joined Angie and Dru on their side of the table. Seated on the other side was Sig Shatenstein and a bruised and battered Shondra Becker.

"Are you sure you're okay, Ms. Becker?" asked Verbius. "We can get the medics in here in two shakes."

Karma sighed and shook her head. "No, I'm fine. Those damn zees got the worst of it."

"Then, I'll yield the floor to you."

Shatenstein sat forward and smiled. "My client has had certain epiphanies this evening. She's decided to follow my advice and seek protection from the Covenancy."

"You realize your possessions, your monies, your property, would all be forfeit?" asked Verbius.

"Even if Rocha keeps her old promise and turns me after she has me murdered, I'd lose all that in the bargain, yeah?"

Verbius spread his hands. "I'm all ears."

"Before Shondra gives you anything, let's just be clear, yes? She does zero time."

Sam chuckled. "You're kidding, right? Have you forgotten the charges levied against your client?"

"No, I haven't forgotten. The thing is, Sam, I know what you do not."

"No objections?" asked Verbius, turning to Sam.

McCoy shrugged. "I guess that depends on the value of her information."

Shatenstein nodded to Shondra and sat back.

"Rocha loaned me out from time to time."

"We figured as much."

Karma nodded. "I've worked in Chicago, Vegas, Boston, Philly, Detroit, Miami, and Akron."

"Akron?" asked Leery.

"Akron. They've got quite a few zees there."

"If you say so."

Karma winked at him. "I do."

"And in all these places, who did you work with?"

Karma grinned like the cat who ate the canary. "In Chicago, Papa Bastion. In Vegas, Johnny the Fist, but Mama Restier was in the room for every meeting. She has control issues. Boston, Papa Petey McBrain. Philly, Big Timmy Johnston. Detroit, the Boss. Miami, Daddy Yngwie. And last but not least, in Akron, Mama Butterworth."

Leery whistled, and Karma's grin widened.

Shatenstein smiled as well. "Well, Verbius? What is her testimony worth?"

Verbius glanced at Sam, who nodded. "Welcome to the Covenancy's Witness Protection Program, Ms. Becker."

CHAPTER 4

THE VERDICT

I

The proceedings against Aida Rocha dribbled on for a day or two after Shondra Becker's testimony, but everyone in the courtroom knew the case really ended in that conference room at Rikers. On the day of her sentencing, Sam came out of the elevator and found Evie, Dru, Leery, and Epatha Van Helsing waiting for him. "Uh-oh," he said with a smile. "Am I in trouble or what?"

"Moral support, Counselor," said Leery. "We're here to cheer when that woman gets sentenced to about a dozen lifetimes."

"Let's hope Judge Sewall has it in him," said McCoy. He put his hand out toward Van Helsing. "And you, Epatha? Have you recovered?"

She nodded, but everyone saw her flicker in and out of phase. "For the most part, I have. That blue horror, Karma, stole part of my essence, but the healer has assured me it will eventually find its way back to me."

McCoy grimaced. "I know the decision to put her in protection probably tastes bad to you, but—"

"To say true, I do feel a little blinded that she won't see the inside of a black house, but I suppose getting her to blow the gab on so many of the high and mighty makes it worthwhile."

"Uh, sure," said McCoy with a quick glance at Leery. "Verbius has already helped get indictments on half of those mafia bosses Becker gave up. We expect indictments on the rest, as well. All of them will be tried in their home jurisdictions."

"Suits me," said Leery.

"And me," said Epatha.

Sam looked at each of them in turn. "Have you seen Verbius?"

"He went in a few minutes ago," said Evie.

"Then perhaps we should join him?"

As a group, they turned and made their way to the courtroom, and then up to the bar. Sam went through and sat next to Verbius, while the police officers took the first row in the gallery behind the prosecution table.

Mama Rocha was brought in a few moments later and ushered over to join Sig Shatenstein at the defense table. She looked haggard and more than a little unkempt but had it together enough to glare at Leery as she shuffled over.

Leery's mouth twisted in a crooked smile, and he tossed her a wink.

"Don't think this is the end of it, wolf."

"Wouldn't dream of it, dead girl."

Rocha sneered and opened her mouth to retort, but Shatenstein's hand on her elbow drew her attention. She glared down at the offending appendage. "Remove it!"

"This won't help, Aida," said Sig. "Come on, turn around and ignore him."

She jerked her arm away from his, and as he sighed, she narrowed her eyes at him. She leaned close and whispered in his ear, and whatever it was she said, it made the blood leave Shatenstein's face in a rush.

The bailiff thumped the butt of his spear on the floor and called the court to order. Judge Sewall floated in and took his place. He glared at Rocha for a moment, then turned his gaze to the gallery. "Good," he murmured. "I assume I can count on the New York Police Department to maintain the composure of this court?" Without waiting for a reply, he turned to Aida Rocha and fixed her with a freezing glance and hellfires raged in his eyes. "Let's get on with this, shall we?"

Rocha rolled her eyes and shook her head.

"Aida Rocha, having been found guilty by a jury of your peers, I shall impart your sentence. For the egregious acts that led to your convictions under the Theurgist Influenced Cabalistic Organization Covenant, and as per the legislation itself, I sentence you to twenty years per count, and there are thirteen of them, to be served consecutively. Further, concerning the two charges of conspiracy to commit magical murder in the first degree, I sentence you to one lifetime per count. Consecutive." He paused to glare at Rocha for a moment, then continued. "On the charge of using mind magic without the proper licensure, I hereby order you to pay a fine of one hundred million dollars, a portion of which will be used to pay for your incarceration, and another portion of which will be used to make restitution to your victims. In addition, I sentence you to ten years—also to be served consecutively to your other charges. On the counts of conspiracy to commit psychic assault in the first degree, I sentence you to the maximum time available to me under the law. Two lifetimes—and given the nature of your victims, count yourself lucky I can't give you more. Finally, you've been found guilty of thirty-seven counts of holding rare magical creatures against their will and in violation of the Rare Creatures Covenant. Each count carries a maximum of five years, and I, indeed, sentence you to thirty-seven consecutive sentences of five years. I also impose a grand total of three million seven hundred five thousand dollars. All told, I sentence you to ten lifetimes plus thirty-five years and fines totaling one hundred three million seven hundred five thousand dollars, to be collected from the proceeds of the seizure of your funds, real property, and any other damn thing they can find." He narrowed his eyes. "I find your lack of remorse distasteful in the extreme, young lady, and I hope this sentence imprints upon you the seriousness of your deeds, as well as the value of a contrite spirit and a willingness to mend your ways. Your sentence—"

"Well, I'll tell you, you old fart. I don't give a damn about this sentence. I have all the time in the world. You're a ghost, and you might think you are beyond my ability to touch you, but that's where you're wrong. I have my ways. Ask Oriscoe. I'll have my revenge on the lot of you. And that traitorous bitch, Karma, too. You will pay the price for this kangaroo court. You will all suffer, while I'll be living like a queen, with my every whim met, my every desire granted. You think your dungeon scares me? Ha! I'll be running the damn place by the end of the week. You wait and see!"

Sewall threw back his head and laughed. "That's where *you* are wrong, Ms. Rocha. You should have let me finish, so as to avoid making such a fool out of yourself. Given the nature of your crimes, your unwillingness to assist in the prosecution of others, and your threats against everyone in this court, I direct the Covenancy Department of Dungeons to hold you in the deepest depths of one of the Supermax dungeons located at the department's discretion. I further order that Special Treatment Provision of the Canon and Covenants be enacted in your case, and that you be held in utter isolation, warded against psychic communication, with no mail or phone privileges for the entirety of your sentence. You will be allowed two personal grooming hours per week, and three one-hour periods of exercise in the deepest recreation area of the dungeon. The rest of your time, young miss, will be served in a six-foot by four-foot cell without windows, without electronics, without, well, *anything* not to put too fine a point on it." He grinned at her, and it was easy to imagine the man sentencing young women and girls in Salem to the stake. "But please do try to 'reach out and touch me,' as you promised. It will be amusing to watch your attempts." He grabbed his gavel and crashed it down on the sound block. "Court is in recess," he said and waved to the bailiffs to take Rocha in hand. "Have a nice time, Madame Rocha." He disappeared without a sound, leaving the courtroom in stunned silence.

CHAPTER 5

THE END

I

After the bailiffs managed to get the screaming and frothing Aida Rocha out of the courtroom, Evie, Dru, Leery, Epatha, Sam, and Verbius stood in a loose knot, the police still in the gallery with the magisters on the other side of the bar. "All in all, a most satisfying sentencing," said Verbius.

"I especially liked the part where Mama Rocha thought she was all badass, and Judge Sewall corrected her assumptions," said Dru.

"It does have a certain poetry," said Van Helsing.

"I knew the old bastard had it in him, but he seemed to positively relish the dressing down," said Verbius.

"Never mess with a man with a reputation for burning people at the stake with the slightest of evidence," said Sam.

"Uh, yeah..." said Leery.

"I said 'slightest of evidence,' Oriscoe. All of my capital cases had a preponderancy when it comes to evidence of guilt."

"Either way, I think the statement stands without equivocation," said Verbius. "I'm glad to have had you at my table this time."

"We make a good team," Sam replied.

"Think we need to take her threats seriously?" asked Evie in a pensive tone. "I mean, this plot to get Oriscoe ran pretty deep."

"Not as deep as our counter-plot," said Leery with a grin for Dru. "Remind me to send your mother and father a thank-you card."

Verbius' smile quirked a little toward the perplexed. "Who are your parents?"

For a moment, the silence in the courtroom swelled toward the uncomfortable. Then Sam patted Verbius on the shoulder. "Her mother is a practical expert in archaic forms of magic. You wouldn't know her. Come on." He waved his free hand to include everyone. "Before The Bar is right across the street, and I'm treating everyone to twelve-year-old single malt. It's time to celebrate."

As the others laughed and headed toward the elevators, Leery saw Dru hanging back, eyes downcast. "Hey, what's the matter, Princess?"

"Don't call me that in public, Leery," she said absently.

"Right. What's got your lip in the dirt?"

She shook her head and forced a chuckle. "It's...nothing. I'm being silly, is all."

"Want to let me in on the joke, then? I love a good laugh."

She shook her head again. "Come on, before the scotch is all gone."

"Dru," he said in a voice she could barely hear.

"Yes, Leery?"

"I..." His throat convulsed in a harsh swallow as she met his gaze. Her eyes seemed filled with all the light of the springtime sun. "I..." He shook his head and plastered a smile on his face. "I wanted to thank you for believing in me."

She stepped closer and tilted her head back to look up into his eyes. "Of course. I *know* you, Lerome Oriscoe, and I know what you are and what you aren't capable of."

"Oh..." He had to clear his throat to continue. "Do you?"

She smiled in that way he'd been noticing a lot in the past few weeks—that way that made his knees weak and his stomach feel like it had disappeared down a deep well. "Yeah, I do, Leery. We're partners, right?"

"Yeah, that's right." Leery swept his hand across his forehead, wiping away the slick sweat that had beaded there. "Partners. But, Dru, if that were to change..."

"I know, Leery," she said. "I know. Come on, I'll let you buy me a drink after Sam."

"My pleasure, partner."

Dru answered with a smile that was soft and delightful, and, perhaps, a little sad. Leery slung his arm around her shoulder in a friendly way, and together, they walked to the elevators.

I hope you've enjoyed this episode of CLAW & WARDER and are chomping at the bit to get on to the next. *Silkie Stalkings: CLAW & WARDER Episode 4* can be found here: https://ehv4.us/4cw4.

If you've enjoyed this novel, please consider joining my Readers Group by visiting https://ehv4.us/join. Or follow me on BookBub by visiting my profile page there: https://ehv4.us/bbub.

For my complete bibliography, please visit: https://ehv4.us/bib.

Books these days succeed or fail based on the strength of their reviews. I hope you will consider leaving a review—as an independent author, I could use your help. It's easy (I promise). You can leave your review by clicking on this link: https://ehv4.us/2revcw3.

<u>AUTHOR'S NOTE</u>

Mitzvah was written in its entirety during the Great Self Isolation and Quarantine of 2020 (due to the COVID-19 pandemic). It is (I'm still in isolation as I write this) a very strange time—a time in which Facebook posts by strangers who profess their secret knowledge are given more weight than statements from the CDC, virologists, and epidemiologists. A time where our governments insist that alcohol and landscaping are essential to survival, but that education, the arts, even libraries are not. A time in which strange things are valued above all others: toilet paper, toothpaste, hand sanitizer, latex or nitrile gloves, and the strangely unavailable N95 respirators all come to mind.

Of course, it's also a time defined by the heroism of our healthcare, police, fire, and other public servants who kept right on working, risking their own health to try to fight this thing on the front lines. But it's also been a time of great humor, creativity, and philanthropy. I've seen free concerts streamed over the internet, many books available for free or at greatly reduced prices, many, many internet videos expressing humor and creativity, and a neat attempt to beat back some of the negativity by actor John Krasinski with his SGN (Some Good News) videos (please see his page: https://fb.me/JohnKrasinski).

I'd love to say it's been a time free of partisan politics and strange conspiracy theories, but, alas, people are still people. But it has also been a time when more people have taken a stand against such things than in the past, and that gives me hope.

All of this has impacted the story I've told in *Mitzvah*, and to be honest, what I've just finished is pretty far afield from what I thought it would be. The term *mitzvah* is one of those great words with multiple layers of meaning, but I suppose I should start at the top, so to speak, where *mitzvah* simply means "commandment of God" and the "performing of a moral deed within one's religious duty." But my favorite definition is Merriam Webster's second definition: "a meritorious or charitable act."

So, yes, I wrote *Mitzvah* in a time of great *mitzvahs* (or *mitzvoth*) by people from every stratum of society. That has a pleasant poetry to it, I think. I hope that, when this crisis has passed, we can retain some of this desire to "do a *mitzvah*" for our brothers and sisters of every faith, race, creed, color, orientation, body size, age, cooking style, hair color, political party, underwear preference, and personal pronoun. After all, COVID-19 doesn't seem to care a whit about those distinctions, so maybe it's time we give them up as well.

Please do a *mitzvah* for me. Help someone in need, whether it's as simple as the lovely woman in the Chik-Fil-A in Greece, NY, who left her dinner to move a few chairs for the wheelchair-bound author last December, or as courageous as standing up for a target of hatred—which is another horrible pandemic we aren't doing enough to eradicate.

Pardon me for getting so intense on you. I don't plan these notes, but given my personality and what I value, they are usually more lighthearted than this. I'm going to blame it on the times.

Well, that and the fact that I picked this week to quit sniffing glue!

I say it often: I love hearing from people who read my work. Please allow me to invite you to visit my Facebook page located at https://fb.me/erikhenryvick or my Readers'

Group at https://ehv4.us/fbog, if you haven't already, and to thank you for the warmth and entertainment if you have!

ABOUT THE AUTHOR

Erik Henry Vick is an author who happens to be disabled by an autoimmune disease (also known as his Personal Monster™). He writes to hang on to the few remaining shreds of his sanity. His current favorite genres to write are dark fantasy and horror.

He lives in Western New York with his wife, Supergirl; their son; a Rottweiler named after a god of thunder; and two extremely psychotic cats. He fights his Personal Monster™ daily with humor, pain medicine, and funny T-shirts.

Erik has a B.A. in Psychology, an M.S.C.S., and a Ph.D. in Artificial Intelligence. He has worked as a criminal investigator for a state agency, a college professor, a C.T.O. for an international software company, and a video game developer.

He'd love to hear from you on social media:

Blog: https://erikhenryvick.com
Twitter: https://twitter.com/BerserkErik
Facebook: https://fb.me/erikhenryvick
Amazon author pages:
   USA: https://ehv4.us/amausa
   UK: https://ehv4.us/amauk
Goodreads Author Page: https://ehv4.us/gr
BookBub Author Profile: http://ehv4.us/bbub

Made in the USA
Middletown, DE
07 March 2023